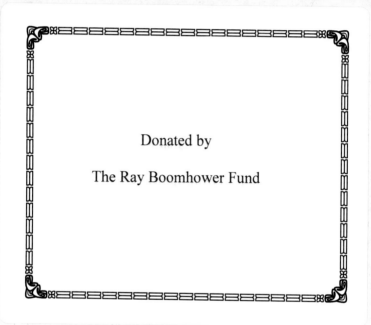

AL**O**NE

THE
JOURNEY
OF THE
BOY
SIMS

ALONE

THE JOURNEY OF THE BOY SIMS

Alan K. Garinger

Indiana Historical Society Press
Indianapolis 2008

Printed in Canada

This book is a publication of the
Indiana Historical Society Press
Eugene and Marilyn Glick Indiana History Center
450 West Ohio Street
Indianapolis, Indiana 46202-3269 USA
www.indianahistory.org
Telephone orders 1-800-447-1830
Fax orders 1-317-234-0562
Online orders @ shop.indianahistory.org

Photo credits for front cover: illustration based on image from iStockphoto.com

The paper in this publication meets the minimum requirements of
American National Standard for Information Sciences—Permanence of Paper for
Printed Library Materials, ANSI Z39.48–1984.

Library of Congress Cataloging-in-Publication Data

Garinger, Alan K.
   Alone : the journey of the boy Sims / Alan K. Garinger.
       p. cm.
   Summary: While working on a road-building crew in Indiana in 1833,
orphan Joshua Sims is sent by himself to fetch supplies in Detroit, and
along the way, his encounters with Indians, runaway slaves, and the
dangers of the unknown open his eyes to a reality he did not previously
know existed. Includes author's note and glossary.
   Includes bibliographical references.
   ISBN 978-0-87195-266-0 (cloth : alk. paper) — ISBN 978-0-87195-267-7
(pbk. : alk. paper)
   [1. Frontier and pioneer life—Indiana—Fiction. 2. Orphans—Fiction.
3. Indiana—History—19th century—Fiction.] I. Title.
   PZ7.G1799Al 2008
   [Fic]—dc22

                                    2008008241

A publication from the Eli Lilly Indiana History Book Fund

In Memory of
Kathleen Garinger

Contents

Preface: Journal Entry of the Michigan
              Road Survey Party   ix

Chapter 1:   Somewhere in Northern Indiana   1

Chapter 2:   South of Tiptonville, Indiana   15

Chapter 3:   Near Wheeling, Virginia   27

Chapter 4:   On the Trail to Fort Wayne   41

Chapter 5:   In the Wilderness   53

Chapter 6:   The Sims Homestead   67

Chapter 7:   On Saint Joseph Road   79

Chapter 8:   Onward to Fort Defiance   91

Chapter 9:   Home on the Indiana Prairie   103

Chapter 10:   In a Trader's Cabin in Western Ohio   119

Chapter 11:   Port Lawrence, Ohio, on Lake Erie   133

Chapter 12:   On the Sauk Trail in Southern Michigan   147

Afterword: Finding the Truth in Sims's Story   161

Glossary   167

Acknowledgments   175

Selected Bibliography   177

Maps

Early Routes of Transportation   9

Map of Indiana, 1830   72

Map of Ohio, Indiana, and Michigan   151

Preface

MONDAY, OCTOBER 28, 1833
Journal Entry of the Michigan Road Survey Party

October 28, 1833—The boy Sims, in charge of general items, was sent to Detroit today to secure ink to replenish our supply lost in a recent but minor accident during a crossing of the Tippecanoe River. We expect him back in 28 to 31 days. Being a youthful and resourceful as well as an agile lad, he should make the trek in less time and in case he does not return in the allotted period, we shall send forth a search party.

Ink: a simple mixture of carbon black, iron salts, and gum Arabic. So simple, yet so mighty, that the lack of it threatened to stall the completion of the artery north, the Michigan Road, in the young state of Indiana. Without ink—permanent ink that would last for hundreds of years—the survey team, a critical part of the road-building crew, could not function. Maps could not be drawn.

Reports, journals, and survey and scientific records could not be kept.

No supply wagons would reach the road-building crew until spring. It was up to thirteen-year-old Joshua Sims to get the ink and bring it back.

1

Somewhere in Northern Indiana

The morning after the accident, Sims searched the swollen river for miles downstream, looking for supplies that might have survived. Except for two small casks of lamp oil, he found nothing. Most of the supplies had been retrieved from the swirling water immediately after the canoe overturned, but the paper packets of dried ink merely dissolved in the water and were lost. Sims followed the river to where it curved sharply north and then returned to the base camp.

It had been an unusual fall. Except for a brief cold snap, just enough to turn the leaves to brilliant reds and golds, it had been an extremely hot October. They called it Indian summer and cursed the misery it brought. The rain two nights before had offered no relief. It merely produced sticky mud and awakened the insects in the steamy swamps. The soggy ground mired the horses' hooves. Men dripped with sweat as their overheated animals strained at their loads, often falling, only rising at the loud and profane urging of the drivers.

It was nearly noon by the time Sims got back to the base camp. He removed the long-handled dipper from its wire hook on the water wagon, opened the spigot, and filled the dipper. He drank deeply, heedless of the excess water that missed his mouth and dripped off his chin. He pulled off his deerskin cap and poured the remaining water on his head. It dribbled through his curly black hair and soaked his coarse shirt. He filled the dipper again and, shutting his brown eyes, threw the water directly into his face. He returned the dipper and ran his callused hands over his sun-tanned face and neck.

Sims went directly to the nearly empty cook tent. Few workers were at the base camp for the noon meal. He dumped a large helping of beans, side pork, and cornbread onto his tin plate. He filled a large metal mug with steaming black coffee, so strong it would float a rail-splitter's wedge, and sat on a rough bench to eat.

Captain Thomas Brown, the leader of the survey team, came into the tent. He was a slight man with a military bearing, a neat and proper soldier. It was said that he could walk across a swamp and not get the tiniest speck of mud on his highly polished riding boots.

"Sims," he said in his official voice. "I've been looking for you. Did you find any ink? Did any at all survive?"

"No, sir," Sims replied, gulping a mouthful of beans and jumping to his feet.

"Tarnation! I had hoped that at least one packet would have survived."

"I found two casks of lamp oil. That's all." Sims motioned to the casks outside the cook tent.

"We can't go on without ink. We can't wait until spring," Captain Brown said.

He stroked his chin and looked intently at Sims. "We're sending you to Detroit to get us resupplied."

"Detroit? Me?"

"We have no choice. Mr. Johnson says we have only a few weeks' worth of ink remaining. Get your things. You leave immediately," Captain Brown said. It was the voice he had used to bark orders to the soldiers before he retired from the military. He still wore the uniform, and the determination in his voice was part of that demeanor.

It was an unquestioned command.

"Yes, sir," Sims said. No matter that Sims had only a vague idea of where Detroit was. No matter that he had no idea of how to get there. An order was an order.

Captain Brown showed Sims the contents of a sealskin pouch. "This contains an order for the ink and a travel voucher. The voucher is a letter of introduction. It can be used in settlements just like money. Shopkeepers can bill the company. Mr. Johnson will give you maps. The maps will list the checkpoints. Be sure you report at each place and that you come back by exactly the same route. Do you understand?"

Sims nodded. "Yes, sir."

Captain Brown closed the pouch and handed it to Sims. "If we need to find you, we must know where to look. Stop at the trading post in Tiptonville and pick up the trade goods I ordered for you. Use the voucher wisely. If you need help from the Indians, the trade goods should do the job. Godspeed."

With no more instruction than that, Captain Brown turned on his heels and left the tent.

Sims finished his meal quickly. His mind was whirling as he dashed across the campground toward the tent he shared with Adam Miller and Mr. Johnson.

Miller and Mr. Johnson were the only people on the road-building crew whom Sims considered friends. Miller, four years older than Sims, was proud of the fact that he had been born the same year that Indiana became a state. His hair was as blond as Sims's was black, a real towhead. Miller and Sims had joined the road-building crew the same day. They had met in Logansport and ridden the same supply wagon to Tiptonville, a short distance from the base camp. That was just over a year ago.

Sims's first impression of Tiptonville was peculiar. He thought it odd that a town, no matter how tiny, should be named after Senator John Tipton, the land developer who was, in part, responsible for his being there in the first place. He was surprised to learn that the settlement existed solely to fulfill the conditions of a treaty. A series of lakes had been dammed to construct a mill for the purpose of making flour for the Indians. As a result, there were Indians in Tiptonville most of the time, a situation that made Sims's flesh creep every time he was in the village.

Miller had taken a job as a hostler, a driver of horses. Sims was assigned to "general duties" as an errand boy who filled in wherever needed. The boys were about the same size despite their difference in age, and they often argued whether it was Sims who was large for his age or Miller who was small for his. They were the youngest of the fifty workers in the crew.

Sims and Miller provided much of the entertainment in the camp. They had an ongoing Indian wrestling competition. Lying on their backs with left legs entwined, each tried to roll the other over. Sims almost always won. He was far more athletic than Miller. It had gotten to the point that the members of the party had to offer odds to get a wager against Sims.

The other friend, Mr. Johnson, was the naturalist with the survey party. He was a tall slender man with close-set eyes and a beak-like nose. He often quoted poetry and recited long passages from Shakespeare. His job was to identify the plants and animals they encountered on their journey and make detailed scientific drawings. He also drew and illustrated the final version of all the maps the party made. This explained his affection for ink. His attraction to the other liquid in his life, whiskey, was not as easily clarified. But nothing could explain his hatred for the native people. It was an attitude shared by most of the people Sims knew—most of them, but not Miller.

Mr. Johnson reminded Sims of his teacher back in Virginia. As Sims went about his daily chores, helping the surveyors, taking supplies to the woodcutters, setting up temporary campsites, he was always alert for new plants to collect for Mr. Johnson.

If Sims brought back something unusual to the base camp, Mr. Johnson always doffed his hat, swept low in an exaggerated bow, and said, "The scientific world is in your debt, Master Sims."

On these occasions, Sims watched closely as Mr. Johnson pressed the specimens between large sheets of blotter paper. Then they both leafed through large books—herbals, Mr. Johnson called them—to identify the new plant. If they matched the plant in question to a picture in one of his books, Mr. Johnson recorded the scientific name and the location of the find, using a goose quill pen.

The goose quill, according to Mr. Johnson, was the only drawing implement worthy of his art. It yielded easily to the flourishes that embellished his work. Sims admired Mr. Johnson's stylized artistic penmanship.

Mr. Johnson looked up from his drawing table as Sims entered the tent.

"I have to go to Detroit to get some more papers of ink. Captain Brown just gave me the order," Sims said.

"I know about Detroit. The captain and I talked about it last night. We decided that you were the best one to make the trip. If you had found any at all, it might not have been necessary."

"Didn't find a single paper."

"Well, at least you'll be traveling mostly through settled country. You won't have to deal with the Indians until you get north of Fort Wayne," Mr. Johnson said.

Sims opened the small trunk at the foot of his bunk and removed his father's "possibles bag." He checked the contents: a small rosewood box, the only remembrance he had of his mother; a compass his uncle had given him; his father's tinderbox; and a deerskin pouch that contained his life's savings, twenty-two dollars and seventy-four cents. He tossed the money pouch in his hand twice and smiled. Two weeks before, it had contained nearly ninety dollars, a huge sum. He strapped it under his shirt. *My plan is working*, he thought. *I will keep my promise.*

He strapped his hunting knife to his belt and hung the bag around his neck. If it hadn't been for the memories these simple possessions called to mind, he could not have endured his job with the road-building team. If it hadn't been for his promise, he would be with his sister in Buffalo, New York.

He blew the dust off a large metal mug called a flagon. This would be his only utensil. He dumped the contents of a small wooden box into the shoulder bag: a supply of dried venison jerky, a leather bag of ground coffee, and some hickory nuts. He filled his water skin from their water bucket and hung it over his left shoulder so it swung beneath his right elbow. He carefully rolled his blanket and tied it with a leather thong, then lashed it to his belt so it dangled down behind.

Mr. Johnson untied a small sealskin pouch, spread a hastily drawn map on the table, and turned toward Sims. "I sketched this map for you." As crude as it was, Sims still recognized it as Mr. Johnson's handiwork.

The map showed only the locations of a few towns and settlements, rivers, and military encampments. It marked no roads or trails, for few existed, since it was mostly swamp and the area had not yet been adequately mapped. Large circles surrounded the places where he was to report: at the land office in Fort Wayne, Indiana, at the Ohio trading posts of Fort Defiance and Perrysburg, and finally at the federal land office in Detroit, Michigan Territory.

Sims's eye fell on his destination, Detroit, at the west end of Lake Erie. To the east, the lake drifted off the edge of the map.

"How far is Detroit from Buffalo?" Sims asked.

"Buffalo, New York? You're not figuring to go to Detroit by way of Buffalo, are you?" Mr. Johnson grinned at him.

"Just wondering. I have family there. I intend to go there sometime."

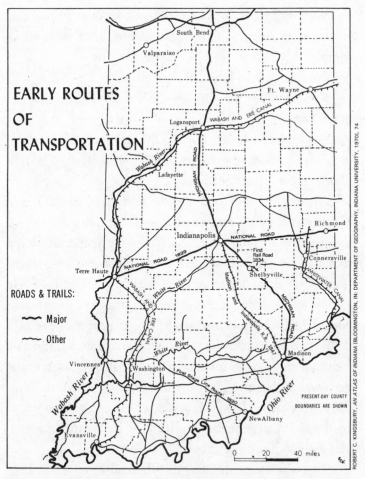

This map shows the major nineteenth-century routes of transportation in Indiana, including the Michigan and National roads, the Wabash and Erie Canal, and the Madison and Indianapolis Railroad. Michigan Road stretched from Madison, Indiana, on the Ohio River to Michigan City on Lake Michigan.

"Well, not this trip. Detroit is only halfway to Buffalo. You need to be back here within a month, or we're all in trouble."

"How far is it to Detroit?"

"Round trip by the route I've picked, about five hundred miles."

Five hundred miles. His family had traveled no more than seven hundred getting from Virginia to the frontier. That trip had taken nearly three months.

Sims studied the map. *Halfway to Buffalo*, he thought.

He put his right index finger on Detroit and his left on the position of the base camp. "Why are you sending me to Fort Wayne? It looks like it's going the wrong direction. Why don't I just make a beeline for Detroit?" He ran his left finger to meet his right, a straight line that was considerably shorter than Mr. Johnson's proposed route.

"That'd be the thing to do if you were a duck. There's a hundred and twenty miles of swamp that way. You'd either get stuck in the mud until your bones bleached, or you'd starve to death. Or worse, you'd get malaria and shiver so hard you'd wear holes in your britches from the inside out. No, follow the course shown."

Sims was unconvinced, but if he had learned anything in the past year, it was to never question authority.

Sims threw the heavy bag over his shoulder and opened the tent flap.

"Report at each checkpoint. Be certain that someone knows you've been there. By all means, come back by the same route. We'll give you a month. If you aren't back by then, I'll come looking for you. Maybe. I wouldn't enjoy wandering around a swamp looking for the likes of you," Mr. Johnson said with a laugh.

"I'll see you in a month, then," Sims said as he waved good-bye. Up to this point, Sims had taken the proposed trip lightly. But just having said good-bye caused the reality of the adventure to strike home. His heart skipped a beat and suddenly his mouth was cottony.

"Be careful those Indian maidens don't get you," Mr. Johnson shouted. "I don't want you coming back here with a squaw."

"Don't fret about that!" Sims said emphatically.

He stuck his head into the cook tent. No one was there. He picked up some hardtack and a large chunk of corn-bread. He grabbed a handful of saltwater crackers that were so hard they were inedible unless soaked in coffee. Just as he reached into the apple barrel and took out two large apples, the cook returned.

"What are you doing?" the cook shouted.

Sims was so surprised he could say nothing.

"Stealing food? You rascal!" The cook threw the dipper he was carrying. It ricocheted off the apple barrel and hit a tent pole, barely missing Sims's head.

Sims grabbed one more apple, spun, and jumped behind a supply wagon. The cook charged out of the tent with a bucket of water, shouting obscenities.

Sims ran toward the road that led to Tiptonville.

He trotted most of the way to the trading post, where he picked up the order of trade goods from the storekeeper. These were some flints for the flintlock rifles so popular among the Indians, some small cutlery, small bags of buckshot, and a few trinkets. He would use them to barter with the Indians for supplies he needed on his trip.

The additional burden slowed him as he headed for the trail he knew was a shortcut to the Michigan Road.

The trail took him down the west edge of Lake Manitou, the lake that had resulted from building the dam, combining the volume of the original lakes. The impounded water, in turn, ran the waterwheel-driven mill.

According to Indian legend, a monster lived in these lakes. The monster was mostly friendly, but did not like noise. If disturbed by loud noises, especially laughter, it became violent and came ashore to feast on children, or so the legend said.

He hurried along the trail remembering a discussion he once heard between Mr. Johnson and Miller about the monster legend.

"It is just another example of the ridiculous superstition of the savages," Mr. Johnson said. "As a man of science, I can tell you it's just a childish myth that demonstrates still another weakness in the savage culture."

Miller, who usually listened to Mr. Johnson but said nothing, became irritated with the man's continual berating of the native people.

"Maybe it ain't so strange. I ain't saying that there's a monster, but maybe it's like the goblin stories our folks told us," Miller said.

"But we don't believe in goblins when we're grown up. I've seen Indian braves going to the edge of the lake with sacrifices to appease the monster," Mr. Johnson scoffed.

"I allow it's just a goblin story. Mothers told it to keep children away from the water. Fathers told it to shut 'em up so they wouldn't scare away the fish. That's all. They ain't any different than us."

Miller and Mr. Johnson had argued into the night. When Miller finally tired of it, he said, "I never seen the beat of you, Johnson. Injuns ain't ignorant. They know things that ain't in those fancy books you keep your crooked nose poked into all the time." With that, Miller said no more.

The trail turned to the west, and just as Sims was about to leave the lake behind, he turned around, cupped his hands to his mouth, threw back his head, and let out a whoop that could be heard for miles. Even if his loud voice did disturb the monster, Sims escaped unharmed.

He spun on his heels and ran at top speed toward the Michigan Road.

2

South of Tiptonville, Indiana

The afternoon sun beat down on Sims's shoulders. No more than two hours into his journey, he removed his buckskin jacket. He walked purposefully with a measured gait, two hundred twenty steps to the furlong, eight furlongs to the mile. It was a skill he had learned from the surveyors. He often carried their stakes for them. With a bundle under his arm, Sims was to drop a stake at thirty-three-foot intervals—two rods. He soon became expert at this task. The result was that he walked the same measured step wherever he went. Subconsciously, he always counted his steps.

"Sims, I swear you're destined to be a surveyor," Ansel Kelly had told him. "You haven't been more than a foot off all day."

Mr. Kelly was the chief surveyor with the party. To him, precision was law. The maps he drew showed his love for accuracy. He guarded his work jealously and carefully supervised Mr. Johnson's final renditions. He wouldn't allow Mr. Johnson's artistic flair to get in the way of exactness.

It was uncanny, Sims believed, that surveyors could walk with such consistency. He often wondered why they bothered to actually measure the distance with their instruments when they knew how far it was from one place to another merely by stepping it off.

Sims had gone no more than a mile from the lake when he saw the tracks made by a load of logs being dragged over the muddy, hilly trail. He heard the shouts of the driver long before he saw the team, huge animals with feet as big as large skillets. He recognized the voice of his friend Miller. Sims rounded a curve and saw the horses straining against their harness. A massive chain hooked to the doubletree tied several logs together. The logs scooped up a curl of mud as they grudgingly moved down the trail.

"Haw, Dottie, haw! You no-good nag, you. Haw, Dick!" Miller shouted just as Sims rounded a curve in the road behind them.

"Yo, Miller," Sims shouted.

Miller slogged through the mud beside his load. He struggled to keep his footing and stay even with the team. He turned and waved but said nothing. He was concentrating totally on maneuvering the team along the slippery trail.

Sims caught up with Miller and matched his pace. Finally they came to a flat place in the trail. Miller handed

Sims the lines, reached inside his shirt, and withdrew a large handkerchief. He pulled off his cap, sponged his flaxen hair, and wiped his face and the back of his neck. He tied the kerchief around his neck and took back the lines.

"I'll be glad when it gets cold. I'd rather freeze than sweat myself to death," Miller said. "Where you headed?"

"Detroit," Sims said.

"Detroit? Why in tarnation are you going there?"

"Ink. We're almost out of ink."

"Ain't they any ink closer than Detroit?"

"Guess not. Where you going?"

"Taking logs to the ford over Haslet Creek."

Sims had helped build that ford. Instead of taking time to construct a bridge, the lumbermen had just roped logs together in the shallow stream and driven their supply wagons across them. It made no difference if the stream overflowed the logs a foot or so. They could drive right through that. However, the unexpected flooding was too much for such a temporary structure.

Miller slapped the lines on the rumps of his horses to urge them up a small hill. The team responded; their muscles rippled and the harness groaned. The boys ran beside the load to keep up with the animals. They crested the hill, but the other side was steep and rutted. The load slid forward in the slick mud, threatening to overtake the horses.

"Huddup!" Miller shouted. Trying to keep the chain taut against the load, he yelled at the horses again and smacked their rumps. Despite his encouragement, the team could not go as fast as the sliding logs. The chain slackened. Relieved of their load, the horses surged forward, nearly pulling Miller down. They were running far too fast when the load snagged a stump in the middle of the trail. The load jolted to a stop, but the horses kept going.

The chain snapped tight. Its links wrenched apart, lashing out like a cracking whip. The lethal tip caught Miller across the back and shoulders. The impact sent him reeling off the trail, where he stumbled and fell headlong into some bushes. The spooked animals whinnied and bolted.

Quickly, Sims grabbed the lines, but the horses continued their flight. They pulled Sims off his feet. He held tightly to the lines, sliding on his belly behind the frightened horses. Mud splashed into his face. Low-hanging branches whipped his arms and shoulders. Bruised and out of breath, he finally gained control, but not before the team had dragged him several yards from where Miller lay groaning in the bushes.

Terrified, Sims hastily tied the horses to a small oak tree and ran back to Miller. He had seen men have a leg or arm cut completely off by similar accidents. He feared the worst.

"You hurt?" Sims shouted as he ran.

Miller groaned, "You think that was a church social? 'Course I'm hurt."

Sims helped Miller out of the bushes and set him on a stump by the side of the trail. Blood soaked his shirt.

Already his bloody left eye was swollen shut.

"Ain't nothin' broke, I reckon. My back sure hurts," Miller said.

Sims pulled away Miller's buckskin vest. The chain had cut through his vest and shirt as neatly as a knife. Blood trickled from a deep wound on his back.

"Looks pretty bad. Can you walk?"

Miller struggled to his feet.

"I'll hitch the team. You can ride on the load to the ford. Someone there can doctor you," Sims said.

Sims backed the team to the load, refastened what was left of the chain, pulled the load clear of the stump, and got Miller situated on the logs. He packed the wound with Miller's kerchief.

In what seemed like forever, they were once again moving down the trail toward help. They finally reached the Michigan Road. On this smoother surface, Sims encouraged the team to go faster. He ran alongside them, steering them around the larger pools of water and deepest ruts.

When they reached the ford, Sims tied the horses and ran for help. Soon he returned with two men, who lifted Miller from the load. They carried him to the shade of a supply wagon and took off his vest and shirt to treat the injury. Only then did Sims realize how serious the gash on Miller's back was.

Sims heard one of the men suggest that they cauterize the wound. After some discussion, they decided that the injury was not severe enough to warrant such drastic treatment. Sims had once seen this procedure. In order to stop bleeding and prevent infection, the edges of a wound were seared with a white-hot iron rod. The pain it caused was nearly unbearable, and he was glad for Miller's sake that they decided not to do it. Instead, they used a harness maker's awl to stitch the wound. One of the men offered Miller some whiskey to dull the pain. Miller declined.

Sims waited until the surgery was complete to be sure that Miller was all right, then he said, "Yo, Miller. I've got to be on the road."

Road construction during the nineteenth century was difficult and tedious work. Road builders had to clear great sections of forested land and build bridges over creeks and rivers. This drawing depicts Washington Street, a major Indianapolis road, in 1825.

Miller nodded and groaned. "You'd better stay here tonight. Sun goes down quick in the woods this time of year," he said in a weak voice.

"I want to get as far as the treaty grounds outside Chippeway. I'll pitch camp there. See you in a month."

Sims trotted back to the road and headed south. He had to admit that it was not much of a road, not like the smoothly graded ones he remembered in Virginia. Not even like the roads in southern Indiana that his family traversed on the way to their homestead. The trip from Virginia seemed so long ago. This road was hacked out of the forest and swamps, full of deep ruts and sinking ground. Now it was so muddy from rain that even their own supply wagons got stuck or broke wheels on the stumps that protruded from the roadbed.

He glanced at the sun. The accident with Miller had taken too much of his precious time. He picked up his pace. It was a bad idea to be out on the road after dark.

He knew the first trail he had to take to get to the treaty grounds. He and Mr. Johnson had hunted wildflowers there in the spring. It would take him east toward Fort Wayne, his first checkpoint.

By the time he reached the trail, the October sun was setting. The trail meandered through deep woods, with trees so tall that little sun ever reached the ground. The forest was so dense that undergrowth could barely eke out a living. Instead of brush, the ground was littered with years of accumulation of leaves, twigs, and rotting fallen trees. And, to his surprise, it was cold, damp, and uninviting. This sudden change sent a chill up his spine.

Soon the trail came to a clearing and stopped at the edge of a pool of water. He turned and walked gingerly along the edge of a bog. The earth was so unstable that it shook as he walked across it. Trees and bushes trembled as he picked his way across the quivering ground.

Sims was aware of the dangers of crossing such places. Sometimes spots that looked like solid ground were not. Even in broad daylight, people had fallen into these natural traps and disappeared in the slime. Now, in the growing darkness, Sims was careful to stay along the edge of the pool as he hurried through thorny bushes that ripped skin from his face and arms.

A covey of quail took flight just ahead of him. The flurry of their wings startled him, and he stepped from the edge of the pool into knee-deep tepid water. Under the low-hanging bushes across the water, a pocket of marsh gas ignited. Instantly, a will-o'-the-wisp spread its electric-blue fingers of fire across the pool, and just as quickly faded.

In that flash of eerie light, he saw where the trail continued on the other side. It was a mere twenty-five yards across, he estimated. Beyond that, he knew where the trail would take him. He chewed his lip as he considered his choices. Then, instead of following the bank, which would have taken another half-hour in total darkness, he decided to take the risk and wade the shorter distance.

Between him and the other side, an ominous black haze boiled up from the surface of the swamp. He struck out across the shallow water for the other side. He had waded only a few yards when he was surrounded by thousands of stinging mosquitoes. Their angry singing shrilled in his ears. They flew into his nostrils and eyes. They stung his face and blanketed his back and neck. He fought desperately, swinging his arms at his face and head, frantically running and falling, running and falling. There was no relief.

If he could only get across the swamp, he thought, he would be safe from the attacking horde. Finally he crawled up the bank on the other side, but the hundreds of mosquitoes continued to cling to his body, biting him over and over to feast on his blood.

He fought his way up the bank, burst into a clearing, and ran blindly, not knowing or caring where he was going. His eyes were nearly swollen shut. Only a slit of vision remained. He stumbled and fell headlong into the midst of a cackling frenzy—chickens!

"Who're you?" a startled voice shouted.

Sims turned his bleary eyes toward the voice. In that instant he thought he must be back in Virginia, in the chicken house of the plantation where his father had been the harness maker. What he thought he saw was a black woman with a basket of eggs, holding a lantern in his face. How could this be?

"Who are you and what are you doing here?" the voice demanded.

"Joshua Sims. I'm with the Michigan Road crew."

"What are you doing here?"

"I'm on my way to Detroit. I got lost in the dark."

"Detroit? Mercy. They'd send a boy to Detroit? Let me see your face."

"Mosquitoes," Sims said lamely. "Where am I?"

"You're in my chicken yard. This is Mr. William Polke's trading post. The inn is up the hill. Come. I'll see what I can do about your face."

She led him by the arm to the stable and sat him on a hay pile just inside the door. She hustled out but returned a few minutes later. She carried a small cloth bag from which she withdrew a jar of balm to soothe his damaged face. She tenderly applied it, being careful to keep it out of his eyes and mouth.

"I thought I'd get farther down the trail than this. I have a long trip ahead," Sims said.

"It's too late for anyone to be in the swamps. You'd best stay at the inn and start again in the morning after a good breakfast."

Sims instantly thought of the cost of staying in an inn. And the notion of having a hearty breakfast appealed to him. But Captain Brown had warned him to use the voucher wisely and might not take it kindly if he used it when he had just barely started the journey.

"Could I just pitch my bedroll here? I want to leave at sunrise," Sims asked.

The young woman patted his face gingerly with a soft cloth. "I'll check your eyes in the morning," she said, nodding her head. "Have a good sleep."

Sims unrolled his blanket on the hay, but did not sleep well. He itched all over. Dreams of the plantation kept coming back to him as he tossed and turned. He drifted into intermittent dream-filled naps, dreams in which black people kept coming in and out of the stable all night. Even more disturbing, he thought he recognized one of them, a tall slave he had grown up calling Samuel. Most peculiar.

He muttered to himself in a half-conscious stupor, "Is this Virginia?"

3

It was past Joshua's bedtime, and he should have been sleeping. Instead, he had his face pressed to the cast-iron register in the floor of his upstairs bedroom. Something was going on down there, and he didn't want to miss it. A lot of things were strange lately. He had sensed it since the Deans, who had lived in the house next to theirs, packed up and left. Mr. Dean had been the carpenter at the plantation, but he and his family left to homestead federal land in Illinois, and the slave who had been apprenticing under Mr. Dean had now taken his place as carpenter on the plantation.

Mrs. Dean had been his mother's best friend. They had spent almost every afternoon together making quilts. Even though they had tried to sell the quilts in town, most of them had ended up in the plantation house, bartered for debts that had accumulated. His mother missed Mrs.

Dean, but she never talked about it. That subject, as well as the loss of the new baby, was never mentioned, at least when Joshua was around.

If he tried really hard, he could see his mother in the dim light below.

"Mr. Sims is determined to go to the frontier. He thinks of nothing but going to Illinois," his mother said to her sister Martha. In all his life, Joshua had never heard his mother refer to her husband as anything other than "Mr. Sims," except to his sister Priscilla and him. To them he was simply "Daddy." "So that's what it is," Joshua said under his breath.

"If it's opportunity he seeks, why don't you come to Buffalo?" Aunt Martha said. "Hiram's soap business is doing wonderfully well. He could work with Hiram, or start his own harness business."

Uncle Hiram's family had started a soap factory in Buffalo, New York, many years before. Hiram and his brother hauled wagonloads of soap to Wheeling, Virginia, to sell to settlers who planned to move west on the Ohio River. It was on one such trip that Uncle Hiram met Aunt Martha, and they had recently married. After their wedding, Uncle Hiram had given Joshua the compass. "Every boy needs to know where he's going," he had said.

"Mr. Sims intends to be on his own," his mother told Aunt Martha. "He's had enough of Virginia, where a poor white man is not considered as good as a black one. You know he won't join Hiram. Mr. Sims would think it a favor. He accepts favors from no man."

"The offer stands, Miriam. Even if you get to Illinois and things don't work out, you know you are always welcome in Buffalo."

Less than two months after Joshua overheard this conversation, Daddy had sold most of their belongings. What little they had left, mostly tools and cooking utensils, was crated and hauled to the banks of the Ohio River.

All of the family's belongings were loaded onto a flatboat at Wheeling. Their wooden boxes, carpetbags, and tool chests were covered with a canvas tarpaulin and lashed to their corner of the craft. They shared the boat with three other people, a horse, two cows, a crate of chickens, and a bin of farm tools.

Flatboats were cheaply constructed rectangular wooden boxes designed to carry large quantities of goods downstream on the current. Once flatboats reached their destinations, they were taken apart and the lumber was reused or sold.

The two Logan brothers, William and James, guided the boat downstream. One stood atop the cabin and operated the sweep, a large oar-like structure that served both for propulsion and steering. The other stood at the bow and peered at the water ahead, looking for snags or other obstructions. They took turns at these jobs. Whichever one was watching the water studied a book called *Navigator*, which helped people get down the river. The safe channel changed often with shifting sandbars, so the brother keeping the book made careful notes in its margins.

The small cabin served as sleeping quarters for the women. The men slept on deck or took a bedroll ashore when they tied up at night.

When settlers first started going west, they made their own flatboats. When they reached their destinations, they used the wood from the boats to build their houses. Now that settlements were springing up farther and farther from the river, it became impractical to carry the material that far. Many enterprising people, such as the Logans, now charged a fee for carrying settlers down the river. When they reached their destination, they loaded their empty flatboat with frontier products such as lumber and continued down the river to New Orleans. They sold everything there, even dismantling their boats and selling that lumber, too. Then they went home and did it all over again. It was a very good business.

Flatboats were at the mercy of the current, and on the day they left Virginia, they slowly drifted away from their mooring. It was an image that haunted Joshua. His mother's gray eyes remained fixed on the landing as Martha and Hiram drove away in their soap wagon.

This frail woman, saddened by leaving her home, weakened by the loss of her last child, was not the lovely mother who had told him bedtime stories while combing her long black hair. This was not the happy mother who played the dulcimer and sang old songs on winter evenings. Joshua did not know this woman who now sat on a wooden box and wiped away tears as she stared at an empty landing.

"No point looking back, Mother," Daddy said. "From now on, we are keeping our eyes on the West and a new and better life."

For eleven-year-old Joshua, the boat trip was a wonderful adventure. The river was alive with activity. There were flatboats, keelboats, and even rafts. Once in a while, a steamboat chugged past them. Joshua thought that everyone in Virginia must be going to the frontier.

The westward movement was good for business. Towns on both sides of the river took advantage of the opportunity. Shop owners set up their wares at the river's edge. These landings were also the province of river bandits who dreamed up uncanny ways of cheating settlers out of their belongings.

Joshua took in the excitement. The scenery along the river was not at all what he had expected. He had visualized being surrounded by unending forests. Instead, what had once been lush timberland on both sides of the river was more often than not bare, eroded hills. Rivulets of mud flowed down the unprotected soil and colored the Ohio. The orange runoff flowed before them like a river of blood. He was surprised that so much of the woodland had been cut.

Joshua asked William Logan what had happened to all those trees.

"Charcoal," William grunted, tugging at the sweep. "Cut, cooked, and sent to Pittsburgh."

Joshua had expected to see animals of the forests, maybe even buffalo. He saw none. As alert as his eye might be, neither did he see what he feared most: Indians.

His sister Priscilla, fourteen at the time, hated everything about the trip. She feared the water. She turned up her nose at the stench of the animals on the boat. She kept her sunbonnet tied at all times and her hands beneath her apron. The Southern lady she pretended to be could not abide the sun tarnishing her milk-white skin. The hordes of mosquitoes and other insects that came aboard when they tied up each night repulsed her. Even the simple meals her mother prepared disgusted her.

Priscilla held in her heart a terror of the Indians. She imagined that once they were away from Virginia and civilization, they would be at the mercy of the savages. She, too, had heard Indian rumors all her life. She just knew that she would be abducted and forced to live the life of an Indian and—horror of all horrors—compelled to marry an Indian brave. She shuddered as she fearfully watched both shores for signs of this threat. It was a fruitless vigil.

For Daddy, the boat trip was merely an inconvenience. It was a necessary hurdle, delaying him from the new life he sought. He stood by the railing, his dark eyes piercing the haze of the river downstream. He kept his new flintlock muzzle-loader musket across his knees and Grandfather Sims's powder horn dangling on a leather strap around his neck. He had selected a twenty-gauge smooth bore weapon so he could fire both shot and sixty-two-caliber balls. Dangling at his side was his "possibles bag." In it he kept his ammunition, extra flints, a supply of lead, a ladle to melt the lead in, and a mold to form the balls. Daddy stroked his new curly black beard. In his mind, he was already plowing the fields of their homestead in Illinois.

The family's trip was uneventful until they neared the Falls of the Ohio at Louisville, Kentucky. These turbulent cascades stretched the entire width of the river. Because of two nights of rain, water crashed and frothed around the protruding rocks and ledges.

They had learned in Cincinnati that the Louisville-Portland Canal was now complete and could take them safely around the falls, but the toll was so high that few flatboaters could afford it. As a result, most of them still portaged the falls. The boats were unloaded a mile or so upstream, where wagons waited to haul their possessions around the cataract.

The flatboats, relieved of their load, would shoot the rapids. Those that survived the ordeal would be reloaded five miles downstream and continue the trip. Settlers who were unfortunate enough to be on a boat that was lost in the falls either started the oveland trip there or crowded their belongings onto another boat that had survived the rapids.

The swollen river gave the Logans' boat another option. If an oarsman were skillful enough, by hugging the north bank, he could steer the boat into the Indiana Chute and around the falls. It was a risky scheme, since the white water surged through the narrow opening with great velocity. The Logan brothers had built their boat narrow enough to negotiate the chute if the water level was right. They had already proven their skill.

William Logan decided to try the chute. He called his passengers together to explain their options.

"I know it sounds dangerous," he said. "But we've done it many times with no problems. Our other choices would mean loss of time and money. I recommend taking the chute."

For Daddy, the decision was easy, and he agreed with William at once. The others were less enthusiastic, but yielded to Daddy's insistence.

The harrowing ride was etched in Joshua's memory. It still made his heart pound each time he remembered it. Clinging to the rail, soaked by spray, struggling to breathe as the ride took him faster than he had ever gone before, Joshua gasped as the boat careened through the chute, sometimes mere inches from destruction.

Two days after they "shot the falls," a peculiar thing happened—it was the first time Daddy let Joshua fire the new musket. About noon, the sky suddenly became dark, as if a great cloud had covered the sun. The fluttering of millions of wings hummed in the air above them.

"Pigeons!" James Logan shouted. "Passenger pigeons! Get your guns!"

Only then did Joshua understand. Thousands of birds streamed from the Kentucky side of the river. They swirled in gigantic waves and settled in the trees on the Indiana shore. There were so many of them that their weight broke branches from some of the trees. Still, more and more flew in.

The men began firing. The birds flew in such tightly packed flocks that each shot brought down several birds. Daddy poured shot into the muzzle, tamped in a patch of cloth with the ramrod, and handed the gun to Joshua.

"Lean into it, son. It kicks like a mule."

Joshua pointed the gun skyward and squeezed the trigger. The flint struck the frizzen, causing sparks to ignite the powder in the pan. An instant later the gun roared, sending enough shot into the flock to bring down four birds. The recoil brought down Joshua, too, sending him sprawling to the deck and providing everyone with a good laugh.

The boat floated under the flock for hours. The men kept firing the whole time. The birds spattered the boat with droppings, sending the women to the cabin and causing William Logan, at the sweep, to pull his coat over his head. That night when they tied up at the bank, everyone bailed water from the river to remove the whitewash left by the birds. Then they celebrated with a feast of roasted pigeon.

It was something Joshua thought of every day, especially how funny Priscilla was, holding her nose in disgust the whole time.

The final week they spent on the river was uneventful. They unloaded their goods at Rockport, Indiana. This was the jumping-off place for many settlers. Dozens of families had set up temporary camps there near the river as they prepared to head into the frontier. It was actually a busy place. Merchants brought their wares for a final attempt to extract as much from the settlers as they could.

They had carried their belongings about two hundred yards from the river and set up camp. Mother was so tired that she lay in the shade of a huge elm tree while Joshua built a small fire so Priscilla could brew some tea for Mother. Then he arranged their shipping crates so he could throw the canvas tarp across the top to provide a little shelter.

He looked back at the river. The Logan brothers had already removed the cabin from their boat and were busy unloading lumber from a wagon. He felt a pang of sadness seeing his home for the last few weeks treated so harshly.

"We need a wagon," Daddy said to his family. "It's a long way to Illinois." He strolled among the other settlers asking if they needed any harness work done. That evening Joshua spent an uneasy night curled up under the elm tree. Priscilla, Mother, and Daddy stayed in the crude tent he had erected.

The next morning Daddy shouldered his harness equipment and walked three miles downstream to a sawmill. It was a very successful venture. There was almost always traffic at sawmills. Loggers hauled in timber. Homesteaders brought logs that they had not burned, and draymen carted the finished lumber to the river. Most important, people doing business at a sawmill often had money to pay for harness repair. In just six days' time he had earned enough money to buy an ox and a cart. They loaded up their belongings and headed toward Illinois.

This became their pattern as they tramped north. Daddy led the procession, shouldering his precious gun. He sought out sawmills, where he spent a few days repairing harnesses. Then they would set out for the next sawmill. Joshua and Priscilla took turns walking beside the cart, carrying a stick to prod the ox. Mother trudged behind, struggling to keep up, often clutching the cart with a frail hand.

The plan worked well at first, but the longer they traveled, the farther apart the sawmills were. They journeyed north from Rockport, crossing the White River near Portersville and again near Spencer, Indiana. On and on they trudged toward the Wabash River. By the time they reached it, the rolling hills had flattened, and the settlements and homesteads were much fewer and farther between.

Once they had crossed the Wabash, Daddy spent his every moment searching for the ideal place to homestead. It had to have just the right mix of certain qualities: a nearby stream for water, a hill on which to build their cabin, and most

Many early roads were nothing more than partially cleared trails. Even major thoroughfares such as the Michigan and National roads were often in poor condition due to weather and inadequate construction. This print shows a wagon train on the National Road, which was the main land route from the East Coast to the Mississippi River.

of all, land that could be farmed. Even when they stopped briefly to rest, Daddy would set off by himself to explore.

Daddy was oblivious to the hardships of the trek. There were days when they made little progress, days when their muscles ached from hacking their way through the forest. Each night as they sat around the fire, Daddy reread the papers he would file at the land office, papers that would make his dream of owning his own land a reality. One flaw in his plan still bothered him. He didn't have enough money for the land. He was still hopeful that his harness-making skill would make up the difference.

Mother got weaker every day. "This is a God-forsaken place. It's so flat. We can't live in a flat country without God," she said. Daddy, ignoring her, walked steadily ahead. Now they often went days without seeing a settlement or even a solitary homestead.

One fateful day, at a time when they thought the rain would never end, Mother simply stopped walking. Priscilla was driving the ox, Daddy was out in front leading the way, and Joshua was retying the tarp on the cart. He noticed that Mother was no longer clinging to the cart to aid her labored walking.

Joshua turned to see his mother standing in the rain many yards behind them, her arms lifted heavenward.

He called to Priscilla to stop the cart.

"Mr. Sims!" Mother wailed. "I shall not walk one more step," she cried.

Daddy heard her this time, and all three of them went to her.

"Mr. Sims, I am done walking."

"Mother, I will not tolerate you challenging my authority in front of my children," Daddy said gruffly. "We haven't found a spot that is just right yet. We will go on. We must go on."

"Well, Mr. Sims, you may take your authority and *your* children to whatever destination you choose. But you do it without me."

"Now, Mother. I know we're close to the land we want. It may be just hours away." Daddy's manner softened.

"There is land *here*. Flat land, but land nonetheless. I will not move from this spot."

"We will go on even if I have to carry you."

"Do what you will. I will walk no farther." She stood glaring at him defiantly, her fists pressed to her hips.

Daddy clenched his teeth so hard that his jaw muscles bulged. Priscilla and Joshua knew the signal. They returned to the cart and watched from the corners of their eyes, out of earshot of their parents' angry words.

And so they stopped, not knowing exactly where they were. It was to be a temporary resting place, just until Daddy could find the perfect homestead. There was no one else for miles. It was the frontier, nonetheless, and the frontier was where Daddy wanted to be.

4

On the Trail to Fort Wayne

In the morning Sims's face was still swollen from the mosquito attack. He could not forget his dream. It seemed so real. He even thought that he was seeing black slaves from the plantation moving about him in the stable. Even more disturbing, he thought one of them was a tall slave he had grown up calling Samuel. A most peculiar dream.

He left before sunup without breakfast, without speaking to a soul. He quickened his step. Now he was in familiar territory, and he knew exactly how to get to the treaty grounds. He walked his measured step, calculating the distance mentally.

Sunlight streaked the woods. Spider webs glistened with dew, and now and then he heard the coo of a mourning dove. His thoughts turned back to the black woman at Polke's Inn. What an unexpected event, running into a black person so far into the frontier, Indiana being a free state and all. Sims's only experience with Africans was with the slaves on the plantation.

By mid-morning he arrived at the place they called the treaty grounds. It would be the last familiar landmark. He decided to stop in the clearing long enough to rest and eat a little of his pilfered food.

He had first gone to the treaty grounds outside Chippeway just days after he signed on with the Michigan Road crew. It was a Saturday, and Mr. Johnson had asked him to go along to collect some plants. Mr. Johnson had had a snootful that day. That was how Daddy had described someone who was tipsy from too much alcohol.

As the two of them poked around the undergrowth, a small band of Potawatomi Indians had filed into the clearing. Sims recognized the leader as a person he had seen at Tiptonville many times. Moments later, a delegation of distinguished-looking white men, accompanied by a few soldiers, appeared from the other direction.

When Sims asked what was going on, Mr. Johnson scoffed, "Another infernal treaty. I don't know why we bother. The savages are a nuisance. Should have been out of our way years ago. If anyone would listen to my solution, we wouldn't have the 'Indian situation.'"

Mr. Johnson ignored the proceedings, but the gathering captivated Sims. The sight of Indians dressed in their finest, even from this safe distance, made his flesh creep. Sims's lifelong fear of Indians swelled within him. The rumors of savagery carried back to Virginia from the frontier were carved into every fiber of his body. The "incidents" at their frontier home heightened his terror. An image of his mother flashed into his mind.

It was this mixture of fear and fascination that prompted Sims to ask, "What is your solution?"

"Think, Sims," Mr. Johnson said. He set his specimen case on the ground and sat on a large rock. "The savages are an obstacle to progress. What do you do with an obstacle? You remove it. But the government has gone soft on the problem. Mollycoddling the savages isn't a solution. It's gotten impossible since that incident down on Fall Creek."

Mr. Johnson pulled a silver flask from his pocket and took a swig. He held out the flask to Sims. Sims declined.

"What incident at Fall Creek?"

"Some settlers shot up a few savages, and you know what the officials did? They actually took the settlers to court and found them guilty of murder and hung four of them. Murder? How can removing an obstacle be murder?"

Mr. Johnson took another drink.

"From that time on, the problem has required more creative solutions. My suggestion was to bring in a supply of blankets that had been slept on by people with the smallpox. Savages are very susceptible to the pox. Besides, they'd spend their government allotment to buy the blankets, and we'd get our money back. They'd get the pox and the obstacle would be removed."

Sims didn't know if Mr. Johnson was serious. *Surely not*, he thought. As much as he feared Indians, he doubted that anyone would intentionally give them smallpox.

A parade of wild turkeys darted across the trail ahead of Sims. He stopped musing on the past and thought ahead to his first destination, Fort Wayne. It was far south of his present position. Detroit was north. This meant that for at least three days, he'd be going the wrong direction. But it was the nearest settlement he could get to without fighting the swamps. He'd just have to make up the lost time after he reported in Fort Wayne.

Until this moment, he hadn't worried about the trip, but for some reason, a chill now went up his spine. What if he did get lost? What if a wolf attacked him? No one would ever know.

He quickened his pace and reached into his bag for his compass. He had the feeling that the trail he was on was going generally southeast, but it curved and twisted so much that even his step counting and frequent compass readings didn't help much. He glanced at the compass, then turned around to sight a point on the trail behind him.

He knew that Fort Wayne was considered a Miami Indian town and that he was in what was still thought of as Miami country. Through treaties, the Indians had long ago given up any claim to it, but they were still there. He also knew that the government allotment Mr. Johnson had mentioned was somehow related to the treaties.

Sims had witnessed the trading process during the few days he and Priscilla were in Logansport, where he had joined the road-building crew. Some Indians had come to the Indian Affairs Office for payment of their allotments. The traders were there, too. After long sessions of haggling, the Indians left. The traders congratulated themselves on their shrewd bartering. They knew that before winter the allotments would be gone, and the Indians would have to live on credit the rest of the year. This meant that the Indians were at the mercy of the traders year-round.

Credit! Sims thought. How Daddy had hated credit. "Be beholden to no man, son," he had always said. The thought of his father brought a lump to his throat. His head went spinning back to his family and the move westward, an adventure that had gone so wrong. If they had stayed in Virginia, as his mother had wanted, he would not be here now. His family would still be together, and he wouldn't be starting a journey of five hundred miles into the unknown—alone.

Sims shielded his eyes and took a measured look at the sun. Just past noon, he reckoned. The trail crossed a small stream. He continually watched for blazes on trees, an indication that white men had passed that way. He saw none. He knew that Indians marked the trails, but their signposts were subtler than those of the settlers. Sometimes they were as simple as a tuft of grass tied a certain way, or a small pile of rocks arranged just so. He had seen these markers in the past, but they meant nothing to him.

He walked through an open area and then an expanse of swamp. His recent experience made him steer clear of any boggy ground. He checked his compass again and estimated the time since his last reading. Convinced that

JAMES OTTO LEWIS, *THE ABORIGINAL PORTFOLIO* (PHILADELPHIA, 1836)

Many treaties were signed between Native American tribes and the United States government during the time of Sims's journey. This image depicts the 1825 treaty at Prairie du Chien in Wisconsin where peace was established between warring Indian nations. Although no land was ceded to the United States in this treaty, most treaties resulted in land cessions from the Native Americans.

he was going the right direction, he increased his pace and counted aloud, by tens, the steps he took.

He hadn't stopped to rest since he left the treaty grounds. He paused on the grassy slope of the swamp. By his calculations, he had to average at least eighteen miles a day. With the sun setting earlier each day, he knew his walking day was just a little over eight hours. The November days would be even shorter on his return. He figured that the first few days were the most important. The fall weather, except for being too hot, was cooperating. He knew this wouldn't last.

He lowered his bags to the ground and sat on the rocky bank of a small stream. He took out a handful of hickory nuts and a piece of jerky. He cracked the nuts against a rock with the handle of his hunting knife. It hadn't occurred to him until this moment just how difficult it was going to be for him to get enough food. He would have no time to stop and hunt or fish. The supply of food he brought with him would be gone in two days. Even if he replenished his supply at each checkpoint, he could carry only a few days' worth of food.

He would have liked to build a fire and brew some coffee, but he realized that he would have to wait until it was too dark to walk any longer to enjoy this luxury. He pulled off his boots and removed the burrs from his woolen socks. He stretched his toes, pulled on his boots, and trotted on his way, tugging at the jerky with his teeth. Time lost, even these few minutes, had to be made up.

By mid-afternoon, the trail was easier to follow. He had seen no one, but this section was obviously more traveled. Now the trail forked, and he was faced with his first major decision. The trail to his right headed south. He knew he was still north of Fort Wayne. He ran down this trail fifty yards to see if it continued in that direction. He certainly didn't want to get on a trail that led him back west. It was hard to tell, but this trail was not as travel worn. He ran back to the fork at top speed.

Frantically, he looked for blazes or any other indication of which trail to take. Aware that he was losing precious time, he tried the left fork. He had traveled no more than twenty-five yards when he saw fresh horse tracks in the mud. He knelt for a closer look. The horses that left the prints wore shoes—white men's horses! He searched the trees for blazes. He saw none. Still, he was convinced that this was the trail to take.

He glanced back toward the fork and checked his compass. Then he spotted the tallest tree he could see ahead and mentally calculated the angle—due east. Again he marched forward with his measured step toward the tall tree. He would repeat this process time and again, until he was sure he was going toward Fort Wayne.

The farther he went, the more evidence he saw of horse traffic. By the time the sun was low in the sky, the trail was rutted with hoof prints. He thought that perhaps he was approaching a settlement.

It was time to find a place to spend the night. As Sims walked, his eyes searched the edges of the woods. He was looking for something very important—a cradle knoll. Mr. Kelly had told him about them.

"When trees fall down in the forest," Mr. Kelly had said, "their roots pull up a ball of dirt. The trees rot away, but holes remain. A perfect place for loggers to hide from the foreman and take a nap. If you ever have to stay in the forest at night, a moss-covered cradle knoll is ideal."

At dusk, Sims found what he was looking for. He left the trail to investigate. About fifteen yards from the trail, sandwiched between two beech trees, was a cradle knoll. The roots that had produced it had long since returned to the soil, and grass grew in the depression. Autumn leaves carpeted the ground. Piled in the depression, they would make a fine bed.

Sims laid down his shoulder bags. He scraped the edge of the knoll with his foot to remove the litter down to bare ground. He quickly found the makings for a fire. As he struck the flint to direct a spark into the tinder, he could already smell the coffee he was going to brew. "Coffee soup," he said aloud. How much a part of his life that had been. He remembered those weeks with his family, crossing southern Indiana, when coffee soup, stale bread soaked in strong coffee, was about all they had to eat. At the time, he thought he would never want to taste it again. Now, he was looking forward to it with great anticipation.

Sims piled leaves in the cradle knoll and spread his blanket over them. By the time the coffee was boiling, darkness surrounded him. He took two large swigs of coffee, then broke the salt-water crackers into the flagon—coffee soup. The warm brew soothed him. He ate one apple. Only then did he realize how tired he was. He had had a good day of walking, eighteen miles at least, he guessed. He finished his meal, put out his fire, and lay back on his blanket.

He fell into a troubled sleep at once. In his fitful recurring dream, his mother held him and Priscilla behind her. Her frail body shook, and her muscles tensed. Sims was so frightened that the blood drained from his face. Priscilla trembled, holding her arms crossed tightly over her chest as if to ward off danger.

They hid at the edge of the clearing, hoping not to be seen, as a band of Indians rode around and around their cabin. The leader of the party saw them and approached their hiding place. He stopped his horse within inches of them, looking straight at them. Then he laughed, spun his mount, and signaled the others, and they disappeared. Sims always awoke at this point, as he did this night, dripping with sweat. His hand went to his shoulder as if to touch the weak hand of his mother.

His mother had died two weeks after the encounter with the Indians. The harshness of frontier life and the long days of hard labor added to the responsibility of caring for her family had sapped the very life out of her. She had gone to sleep, never to awaken. The strangeness of that morning still haunted Sims. He and Priscilla had clung to each other, sobbing in the drabness of their lean-to shack. Daddy sat at the crude table, his head cradled in his rugged hands.

Sims lay breathing hard as the dream images faded. Stars shone through the naked branches of the tall trees around him. The waning moon cast eerie shadows in the woods. But something was dreadfully wrong. There were no night noises. Shouldn't he be hearing night animals on the hunt? Shouldn't an owl be calling its mate? This strange silence made the hair stand up on the back of Sims's neck.

He peered into the shadows, his eyes just above the crest of the knoll. He smelled smoke. He glanced back at where his fire had been. It was out. Not a wisp of smoke there. Then he saw it—a low-hanging cloud drifting through the woods.

He climbed quietly from his bed and crept toward the source of the smoke. He heard movement in the woods. Looking in the direction of the sound, he saw the glow of a campfire. He lay on his stomach and crawled closer. From this vantage point, he saw several silhouettes around the fire. He couldn't make out if they were Indians or white people, however.

Suddenly, one of the figures stood. He was a tall man, and he looked in Sims's direction. Sims pressed his face into the leaves. He was about to retreat to his knoll when he realized he was not alone. He glanced furtively over his shoulder. Two men were standing in the shadows behind him, inches from his feet. He moved his hand slowly and deliberately to his hunting knife. He rolled to his back. The men rushed him.

One of the men pinned him to the ground. The other laughed and shouted, "It's a boy! Only a boy!"

The tall man by the fire stepped toward them.

"Bring him here," he ordered.

5

In the Wilderness

One of the men grasped Sims's arm firmly, but did not hurt him. Sims was afraid to look at the men, and in the darkness he still did not know who his captors were. Their voices told him they were not Indians.

They wound their way through the starlit forest to a small clearing, where more dark faces stared at him through the harsh shadows cast by the campfire.

The tall man held a lantern up to Sims's face, blinding him.

"Who are you, boy?" the man asked roughly. "Who's with you?"

There was something familiar about his voice. Sims bit his lip and said nothing.

"It's dangerous wandering around the woods alone at night. Come, boy. Who are you?"

"Sims, Joshua Sims," he said.

"Sims, eh?"

All of a sudden, Sims recognized the voice. It *was* Samuel, the slave he had known in Virginia. He hadn't been dreaming in the stable. Samuel had really been there.

"What are you doing spying on us?" Samuel asked. He held the lantern closer to Sims's face.

"I wasn't spying." It was no surprise that Samuel didn't recognize him. After all, it had been two years since Sims left Virginia. Besides, he had never had any close contact with the slaves at the plantation.

"Then tell me, Joshua Sims, what *are* you doing out here in the middle of nowhere?"

"I know you," Sims said. There was defiance in his voice. It was not right to be held captive by slaves. He jerked his arm free. He clenched his fists and stood erect, every muscle taut. "You're Samuel. You're from the Hardin plantation near Wheeling."

A gasp was audible near the fire.

Samuel was taken aback. He set the lantern on the ground and motioned to the two men to go join the others by the fire.

"Did you say Sims? Sims, the harness maker?"

"He was my daddy."

"Why are you here, young Sims? Did old man Hardin send you looking for me?"

With the lantern out of his face Sims could see Samuel. He was much taller and older than Sims remembered.

His face was rubbery and his hair was almost white at the temples.

"Never mind why I'm here," Sims said in a confident voice. "Why are you here?"

Samuel laughed. It was a deep sonorous laugh that caused snickering among the others.

"Why, young Sims, we're on our way to Canada."

"You're runaways?"

"You might call us that. We call ourselves travelers—travelers headed for freedom."

"But there are laws against that."

The other runaways roared with laughter. Sims thought he must have said the funniest thing ever uttered.

"Right enough, young Sims," Samuel said in a good-natured voice.

Samuel decided that a boy like Sims posed no danger. Whatever his reason for being there, he was alone. "Come sit by our fire and tell us about those laws."

Sims did not move. He would strike up no camaraderie with a bunch of runaways.

Samuel strode away. He turned toward the immobile Sims and said, "Suit yourself. Did you eat today?"

Only then did Sims notice the aroma wafting from a small iron kettle on the fire. True, it had been a long day, and he had not eaten much. His stomach gurgled.

"Come, young Sims. Eat. We're fixin' to start our nightly journey," Samuel said. He left Sims standing at the edge of the fire's glow. He reached into a knapsack and took out a small book. He turned again to Sims.

"You might as well help yourself. Rabbit stew. As soon as I read the scripture, we're on our way."

Sims didn't trust what he heard. First, no one traveled at night. Second, slaves were not permitted to learn to read. He started to head back to his knoll, but the smell of the stew was overwhelming. Slowly, he approached the fire. A young black girl about his age moved over in the circle to make room for him. An elderly woman smiled, got up from where she sat, and brought him a tin bowl of steaming stew.

Samuel leafed through his small Bible. One of the men who had caught Sims held a lantern over Samuel's shoulder.

"'And Moses said to the Lord,'" Samuel began.

The young girl beside Sims leaned forward, grabbed a cloth bag, and handed it to him.

"It's hoecake," she whispered, then turned her attention to Samuel.

"'See, thou sayest unto me, Bring up this people: and thou hast not let me know whom thou wilt send with me. Yet thou has said, I know thee by name, and thou hast also found grace in my sight.'"

Samuel read with a hypnotic cadence, not missing a word. It was as if Sims was back in Virginia, listening to his teacher read the daily Bible verse before their lessons.

"'Now, therefore, I pray thee, if I have found grace in thy sight, show me now the way, that I may know thee, that I may find grace in thy sight: and consider that this nation is thy people. And the Lord said, My presence shall go with thee, and I will give thee rest.'"

Samuel closed his Bible. Heads bowed as Samuel started to pray. The girl glanced sideways. Sims had neither removed his hat nor bowed. She punched him and pointed at his hat. Then she bowed her head even lower to get Sims to do likewise.

Sims removed his hat and bowed, too.

Samuel's prayer was long, punctuated by frequent Amens from the group. He ended by saying, "Merciful Lord, keep us safe tonight as we follow the drinking gourd to freedom. And, Father God, watch over our guest, young Sims. Keep him from harm and speed him on his journey wherever he is going. Should any of us fall tonight, Lord, take us quickly to your side. Amen."

The chorus of Amens from those around the fire was a signal to move. In mere minutes, the camp was struck, their meager belongings stashed in cloth bags.

Samuel came to Sims. "Now that you've eaten and listened to the word of God, maybe you wouldn't mind telling me where you're going."

Sims didn't know what to say. He had the urge to thank Samuel for the food, but he was not sure it was proper to thank a slave, especially a runaway, for a kindness.

"I'm on my way to Fort Wayne."

"Land sakes, young Sims, you're too far north. You'll have to take the Saint Joseph Road. Don't miss it or you'll wander around the woods for days."

"Saint Joseph Road? How will I know it?"

"If you feel up to it, you can go with us that far."

Did he dare trust this man? A runaway slave who could read? Daddy would have had no truck with the likes of him. Still, if Samuel were right, being late to his first checkpoint would put him seriously behind schedule.

"You're going that way tonight? In the dark?"

"We always travel at night. There are bounty hunters looking for us. They aren't usually this far north except in the towns, but you never can tell. Besides that, we have friends along the way who expect us to be cautious. Not everyone approves of us, and we don't want to upset the neighbors of our friends."

Sims had walked all day and slept too little.

"How do you know so much about the trails?"

"I've made this trip to Canada many times."

"You're not lying to me about the road to Fort Wayne, are you?" His upbringing in Virginia told him that slaves often lied.

"Well, young Sims. You could ask an Indian. Is an Indian's word better than a black man's?"

Sims was stunned. He hadn't thought of that. There was no assurance that anyone was going to tell him the truth on this trip. Sims could see the others looking in his direction, anxious to be on their way. He had only an instant to make a decision.

"Come with us. Saint Joseph Road is just four hours from here. Miss it, and you lose a day at least." Samuel handed

Sims his lantern. "Go get your things, young Sims."

Sims was unconvinced, but he was wide awake anyway. If these black people could travel at night, so could he. He took the lantern, hurried back to the cradle knoll, and returned in minutes. Sims handed the lantern back to Samuel and turned to join the end of the procession. The girl he had sat beside at the fire laughed at him as he tripped over a log and fell headlong at her bare feet. Pulling himself upright, he began walking beside her.

"Samuel called you 'Sims.' That's a funny name," the girl said.

"That's what everyone calls me."

"Hurry then, Sims, or we'll get left behind."

The girl jogged ahead of him to catch up with her family. Her mother motioned for them to hurry. The nine followers, ten counting Sims, kept their eyes on Samuel. He was clearly a head taller than anyone else. He moved purposefully forward.

"You knew Samuel—from before?" the girl asked.

"Yes, in Virginia."

"How come you're here?"

"Daddy wanted to homestead."

"Where is he now?"

"He's dead," Sims said. He expected the girl to show some sympathy.

"My daddy was sold. That's the same as being dead. I was just five," she said. There was no emotion in her voice. "And your mama?"

"She's dead, too."

"Mercy! I don't know what I'd do without my mama."

An old man ahead of them stumbled under his load. He stopped, struggling to catch his breath. The girl rushed forward, took the sack from his back, and slung it over her shoulder. With heavy sacks over both shoulders, she struggled to keep up.

"And the rest of your family?" she said breathlessly.

"I have a sister."

"I have four brothers and two sisters. Two of my brothers made the trip a year ago. The rest are still in Tennessee."

"My sister's in Buffalo."

"Is that near Fort Wayne?"

"No," he laughed. "It's a long way from Indiana."

They walked silently. Samuel walked to the back of the line to make sure everyone was accounted for. He swung his lantern, checking each face. Then, he hastened back to the front of the procession.

When Samuel's lantern lit up the girl's face, Sims got his first good look at her. She wore a print dress. Its white collar was torn and hanging down. Her hair was neatly braided. Sims wondered how she could keep it so neat, out here in the wild. But it was her eyes that startled Sims. He had never seen such dark eyes—eyes that glowed with their own light. It was the first time in his life that he had studied the features of a black person.

"How does Samuel keep from getting lost at night?" Sims asked.

"He follows the drinking gourd." She pointed to the sky. Sims looked up. All he could see was a star-filled sky.

"Samuel said that before. What is the drinking gourd?"

"It's the stars in the sky. They make a dipper. It points north, the way we want to go."

Sims leaned back to look, but in the jumble of stars, he saw nothing that resembled a dipper or a gourd.

When Sims estimated that they had been on this night journey for more than two hours, Samuel suddenly raised his hand in the air and everyone stopped. They lowered their loads and spread out on the soft earth.

The girl's mother carried a water jug around to the tired travelers. She was a tall, slender woman, and was barefoot. Sims noticed that, except for Samuel, none of the travelers wore shoes.

"How long have you been traveling?" Sims asked.

"Nearly two months. We had to stay in Cincinnati for a week hiding from the hunters who wanted to take us back. Then we stayed four days above Mr. Levi Coffin's store in Newport, Indiana. We were so scared. The hunters beat on his door and asked if he knew anything about us."

"He didn't tell them you were there?"

"Mercy, no. He hides slaves all the time. As soon as he took us in, Mr. Coffin gave us new names, didn't want to know what our old names were. He told the hunters, 'Friends, I'd be glad to help thee. Perhaps I have seen them. Would thee know their names?' But he had no way of knowing our true names."

Levi Coffin was a prominent Indiana miller, merchant, and abolitionist. He and his wife, Catharine, were active participants in the Underground Railroad. Levi Coffin's general store in Newport (now Fountain City), Indiana, was a sanctuary for runaway slaves. The Coffins helped more than 2,000 African Americans reach safety during the twenty years they lived in Newport.

She paused for a moment and stared at Sims with alarm. "I shouldn't be saying all this," she said. "You might tell on us."

"I wouldn't do that," he assured her. He had become fascinated with her story. Still, his scalp tingled at the lie. Of course he would tell authorities if he had a chance. It was his legal duty.

"Well, when the hunters asked for us by our slave names, Mr. Coffin said, 'Thee will have to ask someone else, friend. I know none of the names thee seeks.' So they left. Miz Catharine Coffin said that they were just ruffians from Richmond, anyway."

"Why did you run away?"

"Slavin's no good," she said and took the water jug from her mother.

Samuel had overheard the conversation and knelt down beside them.

"Why did you and *your* family run away, young Sims?" he asked.

"We didn't run away," Sims said sharply. "Besides, *we* weren't breaking any law by leaving the plantation."

"Ah, laws. Young Sims, there are laws," Samuel said, casting his eyes heavenward, "and there are *laws*." Samuel rose and motioned for his followers to prepare to move once again.

When the girl reached for the old man's bag, Sims grabbed it and swung it over his shoulder. He told himself that it was not out of kindness. He was just following

Whites were not the only workers on the Underground Railroad. Many free blacks helped fugitive slaves journey to freedom as well. Their activities were doubly dangerous because they ran the risk of being sold into slavery themselves if they were caught. Pictured here is Billy Marshall in 1910. An African American from Ripley, Ohio, Marshall was a worker on the Underground Railroad.

Daddy's advice, "Be beholden to no man." These black people had fed him and were now leading him to the right road. He vowed to owe them nothing. Besides, he wasn't going to let a girl outdo him.

They spoke little the rest of the way to Saint Joseph Road. When they arrived at the fork, Samuel halted his followers for another break and came to Sims.

"This is your road, young Sims. There's a stream a short distance from here. It would be a good place to spend the rest of the night."

Sims hesitated. Was this man telling the truth?

Finally he said softly, "Much obliged."

"I'm afraid you learned more than you ought to know about us. It's not good to know too much. Can get you into trouble. I suppose, being the law-abiding citizen that you are, you'll tell the authorities that you ran into us."

"It's none of my affair," he said. Sims surprised himself. This time he was not lying.

"Well, if anyone asks, tell the truth. The truth will set you free, young Sims."

Sims turned onto the path that Samuel's lantern lit up.

"There is a settlement about two days ahead. Have a safe trip."

Sims headed south, adjusting his eyes to the darkness. He heard the girl's distant voice behind him saying, "God be with you."

6

The Sims Homestead

"God be with you," Mrs. Thompson said as the wagon left to take her home. Mrs. Thompson, the wife of their nearest neighbor, had come to stay for three days after Mother died. Now she was leaving them, too. The grayness of this November day closed in around Joshua's family.

They still lived in the shed they had hastily put together. The idea that this land was but a temporary resting place was pushed farther and farther from their thoughts. Now with Mother buried on the hill, moving was out of the question for Joshua.

Daddy and Joshua kept the cow and their ox in a crude corral made of saplings they had woven together. They cut and piled the native grasses to provide fodder for their animals. Daddy had gotten a few chickens from the Thompsons, and Joshua had constructed a coop from the shipping crates that had held their belongings on the flatboat.

Daddy had hoped that his harness-making skill would be a source of income, even provide the little extra cash he desperately needed, until their crops could support them. His hopes now faded. There was little money on the frontier. If it hadn't been for the work sharing they had done with the Thompsons, they could not have made it until now.

Mother's garden had been successful, although not many crops could be grown and harvested in the short growing season from midsummer to October. The virgin prairie soil had produced an abundance of fresh greens. Mother and Priscilla had also grown and dried an impressive larder of beans and corn. Joshua had stacked rocks to form a crude cave-like springhouse near their creek. Here they stored their food. It would keep it from freezing in the cold months and from spoiling in hot times.

Now the first snow covered their homestead like a glistening blanket. The prairie winds made little swirls that danced across the landscape like tiny tornadoes. When the sun came out, it was beautiful and restful. Mother would have enjoyed it.

It was while the ground was still white that the land agent's representative came.

Daddy showed him the letter from the land office. He explained why they had stopped where they did. He told the man that Mother's death was the reason he had not yet filed the papers at the land office in Danville, Illinois. He didn't mention the fact that he didn't have enough money for the land.

The man seemed sympathetic to Daddy's plight. But then he gave Daddy the first bit of bad news.

"Mr. Sims," the man said. "You're not in Illinois."

"But we crossed the Wabash," Daddy argued.

"You must have crossed too far north. You're still in Indiana. That brings you under the jurisdiction of the land office in Crawfordsville, Indiana."

"How can that be? I planned to homestead in Illinois."

"Illinois, Indiana—what's the difference?"

"But I had dreamed of Illinois," Daddy said. He ran his hand through his beard the way he did when he became upset.

"I saw your corner markers when I came in—eighty acres I reckon."

Daddy nodded.

"Well, Mr. Sims, let me explain the situation to you fully. There is no need for you to go to either Danville or Crawfordsville. The land you have marked is on property controlled by a private land company in Logansport, Indiana. It is not federal land."

"Not federal land?"

"But you're in luck. The company I represent sells the land in eighty-acre parcels only. I assume you have the resources to purchase the land if it was under federal control, don't you?"

Daddy nodded again. Joshua knew that Daddy kept the fifty dollars intended for the federal land office in Mother's rosewood box, but this amount was only half enough.

"Well, all you have to do is give me that money and it can be the down payment for your farm."

"Down payment, you say?"

"That's how we offer a better deal. It's true you pay a little more, but you can do it in installments. You can't do that with federal land. You must pay the whole fee at one time with them."

"How much then?"

"One hundred eighty dollars," the man said.

"One hundred eighty dollars?" Daddy shouted. "Where am I going to get that kind of money?"

"Well, you have three years to pay it off; that's just sixty dollars a year. What you have now is surely more than that."

"I will not be indebted to anybody for anything. We will leave here and go to the federal land in Illinois."

"I'm afraid that won't be possible. There is no federal land left in Illinois. You have missed that opportunity."

Daddy sat down on a stump and cradled his head in his hands, his long hair drifting across his face. Added to his troubles, he knew, was the fact that winter was upon them. "What am I to do?"

"It's not as bad as it seems, Mr. Sims. You seem like a good farmer. Your haystacks are plentiful. Your family is strong and healthy. If you can endure until spring, things will appear different to you," the land agent said. "But you can't stay here as a squatter."

"A squatter? I will not be a squatter." Daddy stood and looked the man straight in the eye. "Mark my words. If this land is where I must live, it will be *my* land."

"That's the spirit, Mr. Sims. Now, if you will just sign these papers, indicating that you will pay for this land within three years, and give me your down payment, I'll be on my way." The land agent pressed the papers into Daddy's hands.

"I come from a place where a man's word is as good as his signature. I will sign nothing."

"Be reasonable, Mr. Sims. This is the way it's done here. It's just business-like. Senator Tipton has vast holdings. It's the only way he can account for things."

"If this is the land I must have, I'll go see your Mr. Tipton myself."

"As you wish. You'll still need to sign the papers. I'll file them for you, but Mr. Tipton will expect you to pay the first installment within the month. He is not very charitable about squatters."

Reluctantly, Daddy signed the papers.

"Done and done," the man said, folding the papers into a leather case. "I should remind you, Mr. Sims, that though this land is reserved for you, even after you have made partial payment, if you abandon the land, it will revert to Mr. Tipton's control."

"I have given you my word," Daddy said bitterly.

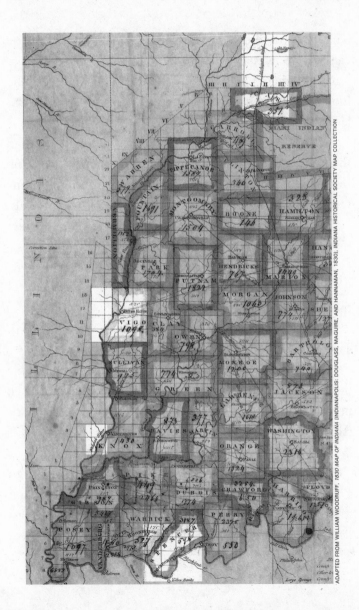

"We'll be expecting the first payment soon," the man said as he mounted his horse. "Good day, Mr. Sims."

Two days after the man left, Daddy made ready to go to Logansport. He shouldered his tools and scrap leather.

"I will stay as long as it takes to earn the rest of the first payment," he said. "It seems that Providence has given us no choice. If this is to be our home, we must all do whatever it takes to make it so." He adjusted the straps on his heavy load and headed east.

Since Mother had died, Priscilla had assumed the self-proclaimed authority of a mother. She used this power to torment Joshua. It was worse when Daddy was not there to calm her down.

OPPOSITE: The Wabash River forms a boundary between southern Indiana and Illinois (bottom, left of map). This map, dated 1830, illustrates this border. Note how the Wabash veers east (right) beginning in Vigo County (middle of map). From this point north, the river no longer establishes the state line.

This is why the Sims family remained in Indiana even though they crossed the Wabash River—they headed north from Rockport (Spencer County, bottom of map) instead of north and west. They settled in the countryside near Logansport, on the Wabash River in Cass County (top of map).

The uppermost part of the map shows Michigan Road crossing the Tippecanoe River. This is near where Sims started his journey. This is also close to the location of Tiptonville and the Chippeway treaty grounds.

"Go gather the eggs," Priscilla ordered.

"Do it yourself," Joshua retorted. "You're not my boss. Daddy is."

"We'll see about that!"

So, when Mr. Thompson asked Joshua to come to their place and help cut and haul winter firewood, he jumped at the chance. It was a good arrangement because they shared the work and the wood. Joshua knew their own woodlot would not supply their winter needs. A chance to be away from his railing sister for a while was additional incentive. The thought that she would be alone and scared pleased him, too.

Joshua liked working with Mr. Thompson and his grown son Walter. Everyone worked at the Thompsons. Even the three younger children had chores. And there was laughter, something long gone from Joshua's family. A standing family joke was teasing Walter about being sweet on Priscilla. Joshua couldn't imagine that anyone could be interested in his sister. They were "people of good humor," Mother would have said. They had an abiding love for the soil. It was an attitude that Joshua learned from them.

Walter brought Joshua home three weeks later with an enormous load of firewood and a burning determination to be a farmer.

Daddy came home three days later. He had done quite well; the initial payment was made. He brought enough bartered goods to get them through the winter. More important, he had traded work for enough oats and seed corn to assure them of getting a spring crop into the ground. Also, the owner of the livery stable wanted several sets of harnesses and even furnished the raw leather to do the job. Now, their simple living quarters housed Daddy's harness shop, too.

Daddy's spirits were raised by his success in Logansport. He worked joyfully by candlelight to fill the harness order. He even sang some of the old songs that Mother had entertained them with on her dulcimer. The whole atmosphere of their lives was better.

Priscilla was more relaxed, too. As contemptible as Joshua thought she was as lady of the house, she was an exceptionally good teacher. The long winter nights were set aside for schoolwork. They had one textbook, Mother's Bible, from which they read every night. Priscilla taught Joshua what arithmetic she knew, always applying it to his interest in farming.

When the spring thaw came, Joshua took to the farming chores with new zest. Even Mr. Thompson was impressed. "Joshua, you are as fine a farmer as I have ever seen."

The specter of the debt was always with Daddy. Joshua realized how much anguish Daddy felt. He had gone against one of his guiding principles; he was in debt and he was beholden to Mr. Tipton. Joshua never let himself think of it except during visits to Mother's grave.

"We miss you, Mother," Joshua said, standing solemnly by the rock pile that marked the spot. "Priscilla can't take your place. Daddy worries all the time about the land.

We don't know how we'll pay for it." He placed a handful of spring beauties on her grave. "I wish we had stayed in Virginia. But I love the land here, even though it's flat. You should see it now. It's green all the way to the sunset."

The cow had gone dry in the early spring. One day Daddy said, "The cow needs to find a husband."

Daddy picked up his musket and let the cow out of her pen.

"I'll drive her to the Thompson place. They have a strong bull. Priscilla, you and Josh try to get along. I'll be back by nightfall."

He slapped the cow on the rump and headed down the path, crossed the creek, and disappeared.

Joshua did his usual chores and even made a peace offering to Priscilla by cleaning the chicken coop and bringing the eggs to the house. At dusk, just as he closed the door of the coop to keep out the weasels, Mr. and Mrs. Thompson drove their wagon up to the lean-to.

It was an odd time of day to visit. Joshua ran to the wagon. His heart fell when he saw Daddy sprawled in the back.

"Priscilla!" he shouted.

Priscilla dropped her bread dough and came out.

Daddy's face was a bloody mass, and a broken leg twisted unnaturally beneath him. Joshua pressed his ear to Daddy's chest. Daddy was breathing. Beside him lay his gun, the maple stock snapped off sharply beneath the lock.

"The bull," Mr. Thompson said grimly. "He's never attacked anyone before. Your father tried to ward him off with his musket, but he was cornered. The damage was done before I could reach him."

They climbed down from the wagon. The four of them carried Daddy's broken body to his bed.

"I sent Walter to fetch Mrs. Gardner. She's wise in the ways of medicine. She will fix him if anybody can. Meantime, we'll stay with you."

Daddy swung in and out of consciousness and groaned in pain. A low, ominous gurgle followed each labored breath he took. Joshua watched as Priscilla and Mrs. Thompson cut away his clothes and bathed him. They put a poultice on the wound in his leg where the bone protruded.

"Do you have any whiskey?" Mrs. Thompson asked.

Mother never allowed alcohol in her house. Joshua shook his head. A swell of fear—clawing fear—surged through his entire body.

"We need something to deaden the pain. Poor man," she said.

"Where are my children?" Daddy said in a raspy voice, barely loud enough to be heard above Priscilla's sobs.

"We're here, Daddy," Priscilla said.

His eyes fluttered shut again.

Moments later he said, "Josh. Josh, I want you."

"I'm here, Daddy." Joshua leaned close to Daddy's face.

"The land. If I don't make it, don't lose the land," Daddy whispered.

"I promise, Daddy," he said, holding back the tears that burned his eyes. "I promise."

Daddy died that night before Mrs. Gardner arrived. The next morning, they buried him beside Mother, near the pile of rocks they had picked up out of the fields.

Promising to come by often, the Thompsons and Mrs. Gardner drove away, leaving behind two sad and bewildered children.

7

Sims walked down this new trail in the dark, counting his steps and watching for movement in the shadowy trees. His heartbeat drummed in his ears. He marveled that he believed Samuel. Even if Samuel was a runaway, he seemed like an honest, God-fearing man. Sims was surprised by his own thoughts. "Honest" and "God-fearing" were not words he ever thought he would use to describe a runaway slave.

No more than a mile after he left the travelers, a trickle of water crossed the trail.

"The creek!" he shouted. "Samuel was telling the truth!"

He felt his way along the bank of the stream until he found a flat place. He dropped his bags, spread his blanket, and lay on his back, staring at the nearly starless sky.

Because he had walked half the night, he awoke after sunup and had his coffee soup, his last bit of bread, and his last apple. This day, unlike the past few weeks, the morning was cool and gray. Sims expected the relief from the heat to offer him a good day of walking. He set off.

As morning turned to afternoon of the second full day on this trail, the sky darkened even more. Sims recognized the signs. Rain was on the way. To make the best of the cooler weather, he broke his measured step and jogged every other mile or so.

The trail now paralleled another good-sized creek. He was on one of his "walking miles" when he recognized a familiar sound. It was the distant clatter of a waterwheel and the squeal of saw blades being dragged up and down through heavy logs. A sawmill lay ahead. His legs carried him toward the screeching sound, which became louder and louder, echoing in his head.

Within the hour, he strode into the first settlement he'd seen since he left base camp. It was just one dirt path with seven log shanties lined up neatly on either side. There was little activity. A woman washed clothes in a wooden tub behind one of the houses. A dog sauntered across the road toward a group of boys playing mumblety-peg, a game in which they tried flipping their pocketknives in various ways to get them to stick in the ground. A young woman with a toddler filled a wooden bucket at a spring. To the west of the camp, three more shacks had been started.

Two furlongs beyond, on the creek's edge, was the sawmill Sims expected. Unlike the sleepy village, the mill was alive with action. Men unloaded logs from wagons. Others maneuvered them into position, heaving them with levers onto a chain conveyor that pulled them into the saw blades. The four blades, drawn up and down by the waterwheel, smoked as workers brushed on grease to lubricate and cool them. Other men loaded the resulting boards onto wagons.

Sims went at once to the supervisor.

"Sir," Sims said, "I'm on my way to Fort Wayne. Can you tell me the quickest way?"

"That I can, young man. Follow this creek to the Saint Joseph River and go south. The river will take you right to the fort."

The man had an odd way of speaking, and Sims had difficulty understanding him.

"What is the name of this place?"

"No real name. We just call it Irishtown. Don't suppose it'll be any town soon. We're on the move."

Irish? Mr. Johnson had told Sims about the Irish. He had worked on a canal project in the East. "The only thing lower than an Indian is an Irishman," Mr. Johnson had said. "They're filthy, profane, disgusting people! Scum of the earth, I tell you. Nothing delights an Orangeman more than to bounce his shillelagh off the head of a Catholic."

"What's a shillelagh?" Sims had asked.

"It's an Irish version of a war club. The only thing the Irish have right is whiskey. Yeah, whiskey is the only thing good about the Irish," Mr. Johnson had replied.

"Is there an inn where I could get some vittles?" Sims asked the mill supervisor.

The man laughed. "We don't get many visitors, laddie. You're welcome to stay at my house tonight. The missus sets a fair table. I'm McDermott."

"I'm much obliged, Mr. McDermott, but I am in a hurry to get to Fort Wayne. Maybe I could just sleep here at the mill."

"A bit rushed, you say. Well, laddie, we have a wagon going to the dam in the morning. You're welcome to ride along if you like. That would get you close."

"Where did you say the wagon goes?"

"This lumber goes to the dam for the Saint Joseph feeder canal. Going to be a big thing. Canals all over Indiana, don't you know."

Sims thought of his schedule. It would be a relief to ride part of the way. He mentally calculated the time.

"If I stay with you, would you take a voucher from the Michigan Road survey team as payment for lodging and meals?"

"By the faith, we don't put much stock in credit here," the man said in a voice filled with high-pitched laughter.

It hadn't occurred to Sims that the voucher Captain Brown had given him was a form of credit. If he had realized it, he would have insisted on bringing along cash instead. That is surely what Daddy would have done.

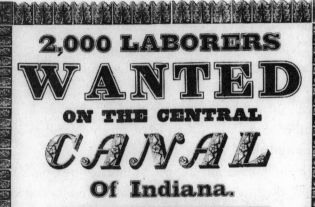

The building of Indiana's canal system required a great number of laborers. This advertisement calls for 2,000 workers for the Central Canal, which ran from the Wabash and Erie Canal near Peru to Indianapolis and southward toward Evansville.

"I have money," Sims said. He thought of his savings, secure around his neck.

"Don't fret, laddie. I'm not offering a fancy, big-city inn and a sumptuous repast. Hotel McDermott is considerably less exquisite."

This man did not seem like the Irish that Mr. Johnson described. Sims said, "Then I'd be much obliged to accept your hospitality."

The mill operation stopped as threatening clouds filled the sky. By the time Sims and Mr. McDermott opened the door to his cabin, huge drops of rain were pelting them.

"Katie," Mr. McDermott shouted into the cabin, "We have a guest for the night. Put on an extra plate."

There was nothing special about the McDermott cabin. It was one room with a dirt floor. A bed filled one corner. A table with two rough chairs and a bench stood in the center. A stone fireplace took up most of one wall. Overhead, a loft extended halfway across the room. As cabins went, it was exceptionally clean and tidy. No, these were definitely not Mr. Johnson's dirty Irish.

"Katie, this is. . . . I don't believe you've told me your name," Mr. McDermott said.

"Sims. Joshua Sims."

"A fine Bible name, Joshua is. What brings you here, Joshua Sims?" Mrs. McDermott asked.

"I'm on my way to Fort Wayne, then on to Detroit."

"That's a long journey. You look hungry. Supper is about ready." The rain came in torrents now, and Sims was glad to be out of it.

The meal was simple but plentiful. The stew Mrs. McDermott served from a large kettle on the hearth was filled with large chunks of meat. It was delicious, and the potatoes tasted like those he had eaten back in Virginia. The bread was especially good, and there was a plentiful supply of butter and jam.

"It's become a tradition that we Irish build the canals," Mr. McDermott said. "Someday canals will crisscross the entire United States of America. If canals talked, they would all speak with an Irish brogue."

"I didn't know there were canals in Indiana," Sims said, as he spooned jelly on an embarrassing fifth slice of bread.

"Well, there will be. You'll see. The state legislature approved the Wabash and Erie Canal nearly six years ago. It's taken this long for the digging to get under way."

"I'm working on the Michigan Road," Sims said.

"Waste of time, Joshua. Canals are the future of this country. You'll go everywhere by boat in a few years. Twenty years from now, if there are any roads at all, they'll just take you from one canal to the next."

In the morning, Mrs. McDermott prepared a hearty breakfast and filled Sims's bag with bread, dried apples, and a chunk of hard cheese. She wrapped them in corn husks pulled from a cluster of ears drying by the hearth.

Sims thanked her and dug under his shirt to get his moneybag. "I intend to pay for my lodging and food. Is fifty cents enough?"

"There is no need to pay," Mrs. McDermott said.

"I have a voucher from the company I work for. Would you accept that as payment?"

"I tell you that it was a joy to have you in our home. Besides, Joshua, I wouldn't know how to bill your company. Just hurry on your way and remember us kindly," she insisted.

"My daddy didn't like to be beholden to people. I guess I got that from him. I have my own money, and Captain Brown will pay me back when I get home," Sims replied.

"In that case, fifty cents is ample."

Sims thanked her again and left with Mr. McDermott for the mill.

"Have a safe trip," Mrs. McDermott shouted after him.

At the sawmill, Sims lifted his belongings onto the wagon. He settled back for the bouncing ride to the dam. The driver and his helper were German, and they said little to Sims during the trip.

At their destination, Sims was amazed at all the hustle and bustle. Dozens of men were working there with hand tools, horses, mules, and carts. Although the dam wasn't finished, it was already a huge mound of trees, sand, and gravel. Sims estimated that it was two hundred yards long and more than fifteen feet high. Its purpose was to hold back river water sufficient to fill the new canal.

From the dam, Sims caught a supply wagon with another German driver, who was going to the new canal's starting point. He was ahead of schedule and hoped to spend little time in Fort Wayne. If all went well, he'd be on his way to Fort Defiance by nightfall.

The wagon reached its goal by mid-afternoon. Sims thanked the driver and followed his directions to the fort. It didn't take long for him to reach the center of the settlement. He immediately noticed the odd assortment of people who lived here, including lots of Indians. Many of the homes were bark houses. Other homes near the fort were graceful frame structures. It was a busy town with wagons carrying supplies and carriages filled with people in all manner of dress. People on horseback filled the muddy streets. The closer he got to the fort, the more white people he saw.

The rain had started again, and Sims was eager to find someone to report to so he could be on his way. He spotted a shopkeeper carrying goods from the porch to get them out of the rain. The sign above the door said "Land Office." Sims went in.

"Pardon me, sir. Is this the land office?" Sims asked the shopkeeper.

The shopkeeper, a huge man in ragged clothes, grunted, "You don't look like a homesteader to me, Shorty. But if you want to talk about land, you got the right place."

Two young men sharing a bottle of whiskey back and forth snorted and laughed.

"My name is Sims. I was told to leave word here that I reached Fort Wayne."

Three other men came in the store to get out of the rain, which now fell heavily. One of them, an old Indian, stood solemnly by the door.

"'Most everybody comes in here sometime or other," the ragged man said, casting a disdainful glance at the Indian. "If you want to leave a message, this is the place to do it."

This sketch of Fort Wayne, Indiana, ca. 1813, shows what the town must have looked like to Sims as he approached it. A large settlement, Fort Wayne was important to trade, inhabited by Native Americans, French traders, and American settlers, and overlooked by the fort, which stood vacant in the heart of the town after 1819.

"I'm with the survey party for the Michigan Road. Name's Sims."

One of the young men unwound himself from the chair on which he sat backwards.

"How'd you get here, boy?" he snarled.

"I followed the Saint Joseph Road."

"North a' here, huh?"

Sims nodded.

The man came threateningly close. "Don't suppose you ran into any nigras up that way, did you?"

Sims was stunned. He was sure his face showed it. The other man wiped his mouth, slammed down the bottle, and came toward him. Sims was going to have to say something. He remembered what Samuel had said about telling the truth.

"Really, all I want to do is tell someone I've been here and be on my way."

The second man withdrew a large knife from its sheath.

"We been following them slaves all the way from Newport. They ain't mor'n a day or two ahead o' us. I think you seen 'em." The man with the knife was now within a yard of Sims.

"Well, I might be able to recall something. What are the names of the people you're looking for? That might jog my recollection."

"You take us for stupid?" the first man said. "Runaways don't tell their names."

"Really, I need to be headed toward Fort Defiance," Sims said in a shaky voice.

"He knows something, Rally," the first man said. "I say we beat it out of him."

The two of them closed in on Sims, but the old Indian moved between them and the boy.

"Going east?" the Indian said to Sims. "Would you have need of a guide?"

"As a matter of fact," Sims said loudly, "that was the other reason I came in here. You wouldn't happen to be a guide, would you?"

8

Onward to Fort Defiance

The old Indian nodded, and Sims followed him quickly out of the trading post. He shouted back over his shoulder, "I'm Sims. If anyone comes looking for me, I'm sure you'll remember."

They walked quickly, the pace set by Sims, who was eager to get away. They had taken only a few steps when two young Indians joined them. Sims felt very odd. Here he was in a strange town, threatened by slave hunters and saved from them by Indians. Now three of the people he feared most surrounded him.

The old man turned to one of their new companions and said something in French. The younger man trotted ahead and disappeared between two buildings.

They had walked some distance in silence when Sims said, "Much obliged for getting me out of that tight spot."

The old man smiled as if amused. "No need for harm to come to a man who knows *nothing*."

Moments later, the young Indian who had left them returned on horseback, leading another mount.

The old man stopped. "A-pi-li-ta will take you to the Maumee. You are a good man, Sims. You did right to not tell those men what you know."

How did this old man know that Sims knew something he wasn't telling? He felt inclined to shake the old Indian's hand, but the man stood erect—regal—so Sims made no such friendly gesture.

A-pi-li-ta nodded at Sims to get on the horse. Try as he would, he could not get on a horse that had no saddle. The other young Indian laughed and finally cupped his hands for Sims to step into. He hoisted Sims up.

Sims and A-pi-li-ta sped away from the fort. In a matter of minutes, they were outside the settlement, riding steadily to the northeast.

Sims guessed that his companion was just a little older than he was. His fear left him as he realized they were merely two young men on horseback, trotting down trail.

The young man did not speak. In the silence, Sims thought about what the old man had said. "You're a good man, Sims." Was he? Wasn't it the duty of a law-abiding citizen to report lawbreakers? He should have turned in the runaway slaves. He would have, too, if they had been thieves or murderers. *People are lawbreakers if you do not know them*, he thought. *They are something else if you do know them*. Now that he had met the travelers, he was no longer certain that a black girl trying to get to Canada was a criminal.

The rain stopped by twilight. A-pi-li-ta reined in his horse under a giant beech tree. He dismounted and motioned for Sims to do so. They sat on a log, and A-pi-li-ta reached into a deerskin bag and withdrew a handful of shelled hickory nuts. He offered the bag to Sims. Sims shook his head.

"I will leave you now," the Indian said. "Follow the Maumee River."

"Does your name mean something in English?" Sims asked.

"It means Prairie Wolf. It is a common name among my people."

"Am I in Indian country now?" Sims asked.

"There is no Indian country near here," A-pi-li-ta said in a forceful voice.

"What do you mean?"

"In my grandfather's time, this was the land of the Kickapoo. I am Miami. Now we live with Shawnee, Wea, Potawatomi, and Delaware. There is little tribal land left." His voice was full of sadness.

Sims felt his companion's anguish and wished he had not asked the question.

"Who was that old man at the trading post?"

"Peshewa, chief of the Miami. Some call him Jean Baptiste Richardville. He is a very rich and powerful man. Also very wise."

"Why did he help me?"

"Peshewa does what he wants."

A-pi-li-ta leaped to his horse, leaned forward, and again offered Sims some nuts from his bag. This time Sims took a handful. Then, picking up the bag that he had gotten at the trading post in Tiptonville, he opened it and withdrew a small drawstring bag of shot. He handed it to A-pi-li-ta. The young man nodded agreement, and in an instant, he was gone, the spare horse in tow.

The woods around Sims were not filled with tall trees like the woods he had been walking through thus far. These trees were sparse, leaving large openings here and there in the forest. He followed a trail high above the Maumee and walked until dark, never out of sight of the river.

Just as he thought he would stop to brew his evening coffee, he saw a campfire. A man was leaning forward to stir his kettle.

Sims approached the man and greeted him.

"Welcome, stranger," the man said. "Come join me for a feast of stewed apples."

As Sims approached the fire, a raccoon scampered away from the man's side. The man was a slender old fellow with sinewy hands that stirred the pot vigorously. His clothes were tattered, and he was barefoot. Sims saw no sign of a shelter.

The man had no firearms, either, so far as Sims could tell. This was not a hunter. A hunter would have had a gun.

"Who ye be, young man?"

"Sims, sir."

"Just one name? No matter. I am Jonathan Chapman."

"Pleased to meet you, Mr. Chapman."

The man cackled. "No one calls me 'mister.' If they call me anything, it's Johnny Appleseed."

The man reached into his pocket and pulled out a slice of apple. He held it at arm's length, and the raccoon returned from the bushes to take it.

"Not much on ceremony here. Do you have a cup?" the man asked.

Sims took his flagon from his bag. The man filled the vessel with steaming applesauce.

"Where you bound, Sims?"

"I'm on my way to Detroit."

"Can't go to Detroit. Whole town's under quarantine. Cholera! Worst epidemic anyone ever heard of." Chapman pulled the pot close to his knee and shoveled the stew into his mouth with a biscuit.

"But I'm supposed to get ink there."

"Don't know about ink, just know Detroit is closed. Besides, we're in for some bad weather. You like apples?"

Sims nodded.

"That's what I do, you know. I plant fruit trees for the settlers. It's a good business too. Settlers don't have time to prove up on their homesteads. I sell them land where I've already started orchards growing, apples, pears, or peaches."

The begging raccoon came back for another handout.

"Homesteading is very hard," Sims said. He remembered the backbreaking labor his family had put into their homestead.

"Settlers need my apples. I bring them fruit, and I bring them the word of God. Takes both to survive out here."

This startled Sims. His mother had said the same thing the very day she stopped walking. "This is a God-forsaken place. It's so flat. I haven't seen a fruit tree for weeks. I can't live in a flat country, without fruit and without God."

Sims was brought back from this memory when his companion said, "Better get a good night's rest. Snow tomorrow. I don't mind weather, but if you need shelter, there's a trader's cabin a day's walk along the river."

Chapman used his bare foot to cover the coals of the fire, leaned back, and immediately fell asleep.

The strange man was gone when Sims awoke. Large, fluffy snowflakes were falling. Sims needed his coffee. He quickly built a small fire. He congratulated himself at how skillful he was becoming at this task. Even with the moisture from the snow, it took him just a few minutes to brew the coffee. He spread his blanket before him and carefully unfolded his map.

If Detroit was closed, as Chapman said, what should he do? He believed that he was in Ohio, but just barely. He dared not go back to base camp without ink. But it seemed foolish to spend more time trying to get someplace he couldn't go. As he studied the map, the whole journey looked impossible. His eye wandered from Perrysburg and on east to the edge of the map. Just beyond that edge, he knew, was Buffalo. It would be easy to give up everything he had worked for and go to Buffalo instead. In either case, he had to get to Perrysburg first.

He was on his way just as the light of morning filtered through the trees. It was a great day for walking, and the beauty of the wet snow clinging to the branches did not escape him.

Fort Defiance, his next checkpoint, was on the Maumee River. He had to be there in three days to stay on schedule. The ride on the lumber wagons and the horseback jaunt had put him a half-day ahead.

Later that afternoon, as Sims slipped in the deepening snow, his thoughts went back to the first snow at the homestead when the man had come from the land office. How hard it must have been for Daddy to agree to buy the land on credit. But he had paid the first installment anyway. It was that debt which had brought Sims here.

Maybe Priscilla was right. Maybe he couldn't save the homestead. Maybe he should have gone with her to Buffalo. But he had promised Daddy that he would save the land. And all he had left of his savings was twenty-two dollars and twenty-four cents.

With the fading light of day came a cold wind out of the north. What had been a pleasant snow shower became a wind-driven storm. The feathery flakes turned to hard pellets of ice. Sims kept his eyes alert to find the cabin that Chapman had mentioned. It was hard to believe that when he had started this trip a few days before, it was miserably hot. Now the wind stabbed through him like an icy pitchfork. He pulled his collar closer to his face and braced himself against the storm.

He was about to untie his blanket and throw it around his shoulders when he spotted the cabin. It rested on a ledge, nestled at the edge of a clearing on the opposite side of the river.

He studied the river, then slid down its steep bank. He would have to wade, but he could not tell how deep the water was. The velocity of the wind increased moment by moment. In the swirling snow and ice, he nearly lost sight of the cabin.

He had no choice but to charge headlong into the river. He raised his shoulder bags above his head and braced himself against the flowing, frigid water. Now in hip-deep water with fifteen yards still to go, his feet slipped dangerously on the rocky, slimy bottom. He braced himself against the current, struggling to keep his balance.

He grasped for a tree branch brought down to water level by its burden of ice. He tugged on the frozen branch and pulled himself to a toehold on the other side. From this perch the bank was nearly straight up, eight feet. He struggled up the ice-encrusted bank. Twice he lost his handhold and nearly toppled back into the river. The straps of his shoulder bags cut into his freezing shoulders. With his last bit of energy, he pulled himself over the rock ledge.

Blinded by the driving snow, he made his way to the door and banged on it frantically. No answer. He knocked again. Still no answer. He shoved the door open and stumbled in.

He called out, but no one was there. As his eyes adjusted, he surveyed the room. It was crudely constructed, little better than the lean-to on their homestead.

There was no fireplace, only a mound of dirt with a circle of rocks in which to build a fire. Over this fire ring stood a tripod made of three saplings. They were fastened together in a point and passed through a hole in the roof. A chain dangling from the tripod held an iron pot.

Snow had blown in between the logs and through the hole in the roof, leaving small drifts on the dirt floor. Against one wall was a pallet made of saplings. Ropes ran to the rafters and suspended the crude bed a few inches off the floor. There was an empty wooden bucket near the door. Traps hanging on the wall clinked as the wind sneaked through the cracks. A pile of firewood filled one corner.

The firewood was covered with dust and spider webs. This convinced Sims that no one had been there recently, and, therefore, it was a safe haven. He got his freezing fingers working well enough to retrieve his tinderbox from his bag. In moments a fire was blazing, its warmth bringing him back to life.

Early log cabins were simple buildings made from wooden beams and logs and were a common form of shelter during the American frontier period. A fire pit was sometimes used, with a hole in the roof providing ventilation, because it was simpler than building a hearth. The fire pit shown here is a re-creation at Historic Sauder Village, in northwestern Ohio, in the vicinity of where Sims found a cabin for shelter from the ice storm.

He quickly shed his soaking clothes and hung them on the tripod. He unrolled his blanket and spread it near the fire to dry. Only then did he realize that he hadn't eaten since morning, and then only coffee soup. He dug through his bag and withdrew the small loaf of bread Mrs. McDermott had insisted he take. He brewed some coffee.

Despite its draftiness, the cabin warmed quickly. It had been a long day's journey, and his recent struggle with the river had exhausted him. He felt his blanket. It was still damp, but warm. The urge to wrap himself up and snuggle by the fire was irresistible.

He settled at once into a deep sleep, oblivious to the raging ice storm outside, the howling wind, the crash of falling limbs overburdened with ice, the mournful groan of entire trees being toppled. Mercifully, his dreams of Uncle Hiram's comfortable house in Buffalo dispelled the cold.

9

Home on the Indiana Prairie

Joshua lay awake in the lean-to, drenched in sweat. Rain splashed in puddles outside. His muscles ached from the day's work. His mind went back to the day after Daddy had been laid to rest beside Mother. How absolutely miserable he had felt. Daddy's words, "Be beholden to no man, son," echoed in his mind until sleep finally came each night. They were still there when he woke before sunup each day. They were his inheritance, and with Daddy's words lived his own promise not to lose the land. These things kept him going.

Priscilla had wanted to leave for Uncle Hiram and Aunt Martha's home in Buffalo immediately after Daddy died. Every day since then it had been the same story.

"I promised Daddy I'd keep the land. We can't leave." Joshua had said this so often that it no longer bore any weight with Priscilla. He knew that tomorrow he would have to hear it all again. He was right.

"You think you can stay here? A twelve-year-old home-steader? You are an idiot!"

"I'm not leaving. You can go if you want. I'm going to stay and pay for this land. Daddy would want that."

"Fine! Then Walter Thompson will take me out of this horrible place. I have had all I can stand. I'll find a way to get to Buffalo." She had packed a carpetbag and started out on foot, Joshua staring after her.

A few hours later, Walter drove a buckboard into the Sims homestead. A tearful Priscilla sat beside him.

Joshua watched as Priscilla flounced out of the wagon.

"I'm sorry, Priscilla," Walter said. "I can't go anywhere until all the crops are in the ground."

From that day on, Joshua got no help from Priscilla. She didn't eat nor did she prepare meals for him as she had every day since Mother died. He had finished planting the field crops with the help of Walter and Walter's horse. He had a large garden in the ground. He had made improvements to the animal shelters. He had set some hens and had hatched enough eggs that he now had a sizable flock.

This Monday morning, he was hitching the ox to a large log, which he planned to split into rails for a proper fence. Priscilla came running. All the blood had drained from her face, and her eyes were filled with terror.

She held her finger to her lips. "Indians," she whispered.

Joshua spun around. He heard the sound of horses' hooves. He and Priscilla quickly slipped behind a haystack.

The old fear of the native people surged back, filling their hearts with dread.

A line of horses paraded single file into the field where the children hid. Neither Joshua nor Priscilla breathed. The Indians were dressed entirely according to the custom of their people. This was unusual. Other Indians they had seen wore a mixture of clothes, some Indian, some white man's.

The tall young leader, wearing an elaborate headdress, looked in their direction.

They had been discovered! Joshua's heart nearly jumped from his chest.

The braves stopped for just an instant. The leader slapped his bareback mount and galloped away, followed by the others.

"That's the last straw. We are leaving this dreadful place *now!*" Priscilla screamed.

"Let's go to the Thompsons' place until we're sure they've gone," Joshua said, still watching the spot where the Indians had disappeared.

"No, Joshua. I mean we're leaving for good."

"We can't do that. You know that the land will go back to the land company if we don't keep it up."

"Let them have it. We can't pay them; they're going to take it back anyway," she said. There was a new authority in her voice. It wasn't the usual complaining, but a sincere concern for their safety. Joshua knew she was right. They had to do something.

They picked up a few belongings, and soon they were trudging warily toward their neighbors' house.

They had been on the road less than a half-hour when they heard the sound of approaching horses. Fearful that the Indians had returned, they scurried off the path and hid in the bushes.

Joshua was afraid to look from their hiding place. The horses stopped on the road directly in front of them. Only then did Joshua peek through the branches. It was not the Indian band. Instead, what he saw caused a sigh of relief.

A troop of uniformed militiamen waited behind their captain. As the leader dismounted, two frightened doves took flight a few feet from the bushes where Joshua and Priscilla hid. The captain's startled horse whinnied.

"Whoa, boy," the officer said to his horse.

His voice calmed Joshua's fear. He stepped out of hiding.

The soldier was possibly the tallest man Joshua had ever seen. He had a chiseled face and very kind eyes. Reluctantly, Priscilla came from behind the bushes to stand beside her brother.

"What are you young people doing way out here?" the soldier demanded.

"We're on our way to our neighbors' house," Priscilla said in a shaky voice.

"Let me introduce myself," the soldier said. He removed his hat and held it in front of his chest. "I'm Captain Eli Turner. And who are you?"

"I'm Priscilla Sims, and this is my brother Joshua."

"I'm sorry we frightened you. We're looking for a band of stray Indians we believe intend to join Black Hawk. We hope to persuade them not to get into the skirmish. I don't suppose you've seen any."

"We did, sir," Priscilla said. "There were eight of them at our place a short time ago. We were frightened out of our wits. That's why we're going to our neighbors."

"Did you see which way they went?" Captain Turner asked.

"They rode west," Priscilla said, pointing.

"Perhaps we can catch up to them before they get to Wisconsin. No point in getting more of them involved in this affair. Could we accompany you to your destination?"

"It's not far," Priscilla said hopefully.

The captain motioned to one of his men who led an extra mount. Then he gestured to another of his men, who hoisted Priscilla onto the horse and lifted Joshua up behind her.

In the company of the soldiers, Priscilla felt safe for the first time since leaving Virginia. Joshua thought that she was actually enjoying the ride. She seemed to delight especially in the attention shown her by the young militiaman who had helped her onto the horse.

A half-hour later, they arrived at the Thompson farm. Joshua slid off his horse. The same militiaman lifted Priscilla to the ground.

The captain removed his hat and said, "There, Miss Priscilla. You're safe and sound. Good day to you, and to you, Joshua." He waved as they left in a flurry of mud kicked up by the horses' hooves.

The three younger Thompson children came running to see what all the excitement was about. Mrs. Thompson hurried out of their house, wiping her hands on her apron. She listened to their story of the Indians, then herded all the children inside.

By the time Mr. Thompson and Walter returned for their noon meal, Priscilla's hysteria had subsided, but her resolve to leave the frontier had not.

"Why don't you and Joshua come live here? We can make room for you somehow," Mrs. Thompson suggested. "All of us working together could farm both places and eventually work things out."

"I don't care about the homestead. That last day, Daddy left me in charge. I say we're going to Buffalo."

"But our crops are in," Joshua argued. "We'll be able to pay up after harvest. Daddy made me promise not to lose the land."

It was Walter Thompson who finally came up with the solution that took the Sims children to Logansport and Joshua to his job with the Michigan Road crew.

"What if I worked your land on the shares—work the land together and split the crops between us?" Walter asked. There won't be much to do until harvest. The two of you can go on to Buffalo until fall. When you come back, we'll be partners. I'll go with you to the land office and help make the arrangements."

"I am never coming back," Priscilla said forcefully.

"Well, I am," Joshua retorted. "It's rightfully our land. Our parents are buried there." *Why doesn't she understand that?* he thought.

They spent the dark hours of the evening going over their plan. Walter offered to buy the ox and cart, investing seven dollars, all the money he had in the world. The transaction pleased Priscilla because this provided traveling money. Joshua almost cried. Selling the ox was like selling his best friend.

The next morning, Joshua helped Walter with his chores, and they harnessed the team to the wagon. They had their sparse belongings loaded onto the wagon by mid-morning. Priscilla sat on the seat with Walter, keeping her eyes constantly alert for the return of the Indians. Joshua, his legs dangling off the back of the wagon, wondered what was in store for him now. He opened Mother's rosewood box in which Daddy had kept the official papers about their land and looked at them one more time, noting the signature at the bottom—John Tipton, Office of Indian Affairs, Logansport, Indiana.

After a solemn visit to the graves of Mother and Daddy, they climbed onto the wagon and headed toward Logansport.

It was an exhausting trip in the wagon. The road was uneven, shifting from mud to dusty, rutted trails. The landscape gradually changed the farther east they went. Soon

Jean Baptiste Richardville

Treaties between the United States and various Native American tribes led to removals of the natives from the eastern part of the country west across the Mississippi River. Understandably, these removals confused and angered many natives. Black Hawk, a Sauk Indian, was one such Native American. The battles that he and his band of Sauk and Fox Indians waged against the United States came to be known as the Black Hawk War.

Although Black Hawk's battles were fought in Wisconsin and Illinois, settlers in Indiana feared native retaliation for the land they had lost in Indiana. For example, in 1826, near Peru, Indiana, the Miami tribes in Indiana signed a treaty with the United States releasing their claim on almost all their land in Indiana, including land necessary for building Michigan Road.

Francis Godfroy

Little Wolf

Pictured here are three of the Miami chiefs who signed the 1826 treaty: Jean Baptiste Richardville, head chief of Indiana's Miami tribes (known to Sims as Peshewa); Francis Godfroy; and Little Wolf, also known as Mo-wan-za. Richardville and Godfroy were both part French, as their native families had married into French fur-trading families.

The paintings of these Miami chiefs were done in 1827, near Peru, following the signing of the treaty. (Images from James Otto Lewis, The Aboriginal Portfolio [Philadelphia, 1836]) they were in deep forest with only patches of prairie, then solid forests, and then bogs and swamps started to appear between the trees.

Each hour they traveled, Priscilla's spirits improved. Walter had draped a tarp over one end of the wagon, which shaded her where she sat on a quilt over a pile of hay. Joshua rode on the driver's seat next to Walter. The bouncing seat wore blisters on his backside, making him squirm to find a way to sit that wasn't painful.

By the time they reached Logansport, Priscilla's disposition was actually pleasant. In this thriving community, there were shops, hotels, and even a newspaper. Just being in a town for a change excited all of them.

They found an inn and rented two rooms, one for Priscilla and the other for Walter and Joshua. None of them had ever stayed in an inn and were shocked at how expensive it was. It was seventy cents per room plus twenty-five cents per meal. The livery cost was fifty cents a night for each horse, including hay and grain. They had brought along the harness Daddy had made. After they settled up, there was a profit of eleven dollars and forty-seven cents.

The next morning they went to the land office. They had hoped to see John Tipton himself. But Tipton had become a United States Senator several months earlier and was in Washington, D.C. He had left his brother-in-law, Major Daniel Bell, in charge. They would have to deal with him.

Walter and Priscilla did all the negotiating. The paper-work took more time than they expected. During the days they spent having the contract drawn up, Joshua wandered around town. He didn't care what they decided. He had his own plan. He was going to stay in Logansport, find work, and earn the needed money. He fantasized about marching into the land office one fine day and triumphantly paying off his father's debt.

It was on their third day in Logansport that he walked past the *Cass County Times* office. Tacked to the door was a recent edition of the newspaper. The headlines told of the trouble brewing with Chief Black Hawk in Wisconsin. Joshua wondered if the young captain who had helped them had overtaken the Indians they had seen.

Just then, Joshua noticed a group of young Indians laughing and shouting in a grassy area nearby. They were playing a game, a form of tug-of-war in which the competi-tors stood on large rocks about twenty feet apart, a long rope stretched between them, and attempted to pull each other off the rocks.

Keeping a respectable distance, Joshua drifted toward them. Standing on one rock was a blond white boy. He was so expert at the game that, time after time, he successfully dethroned his Indian opponents.

Joshua tried to discover the boy's strategy. He wasn't nearly as big or as strong as his Indian challengers. Yet he won every time. The group finally lost interest in the game, and the Indians wandered off. The blond young man threw himself on the ground under the elm tree where Joshua was sitting.

"You're very good at that game," Joshua said.

"It's timing and trickery, not strength," he replied. "It's mountain man tug-of-war. I should be good. I'm a mountain man from Tennessee. Adam Miller's the name."

"Joshua Sims. How come you're in Indiana?"

"Lookin' for work. How about you?"

Joshua's mind said *I'm on my way to Buffalo*, but his mouth said, "I'm looking for work, too."

"They're hiring for the crew building a road to Michigan. Four bits a day and board, I hear."

Joshua quickly calculated. He needed one hundred twenty dollars—less than a year at that salary.

"How do you get such a job?" he asked. His mind reeled at the prospect of accumulating such a huge sum.

"The man will be back tomorrow morning, if you're a mind to do it."

"You bet I am. Where do I go?"

"Right here. A wagon will be here to take the workers north," Miller said. He rose, dusted off the seat of his pants, and trotted away.

"I'll see you tomorrow," Joshua called after him.

He walked back to the inn. His head was full of possibilities. There was now a chance, a slim one, but a chance, that he could make good on his promise to Daddy.

Walter was sitting in a rocking chair on the veranda.

"What have you done today?" Walter asked.

"Nothing. Just walked around town," Joshua said.

"It appears they are going to allow us to become partners. I promised them the entire fall harvest as the next payment. We'll see what happens after that," Walter reported.

"You're not in this alone, Walter. I'll hold up my end of the bargain," Joshua said.

"I know you will, Josh. We learned something interesting. I'll tell you because I believe Priscilla won't. That man lied to your pa. Federal land is still available, not that it makes any difference now."

"You mean we could have gotten land in Illinois?"

"That's what the man said. It's just as well. Where we are, we have a start. That may be more important. We can make it, Josh."

Joshua was stunned. If they had left when the land agent first arrived, they would have a start in Illinois by now. Maybe Daddy wouldn't have been gored by the bull, and Joshua wouldn't be facing the world alone.

When morning came, Joshua left the inn before Walter awoke. He hurried back to the elm tree and, just as Adam Miller had told him, a supply wagon was there. On the side were the words "Michigan Road."

He approached three men who were brewing their morning coffee over a small fire.

"I'm looking for work," he said boldly. A lump in his throat made him squeak the last word.

"What can you do, young man?" one of the men asked.

"I'm strong, and I'm a hard worker. I will do whatever I'm told."

"That's the right attitude. You know that you have to sign on for the entire remainder of the project, though. Ain't easy living in the wild. You work twelve hours a day, six—sometimes seven—days a week. Skip out, and you lose your bonus," the man said.

"Bonus?" Joshua asked.

"We pay fifty cents a day, but only at the end of the job. You get just half what you've earned each week."

The lump in his throat grew larger. "I'm not a quitter. If you hire me, I'll do what I promise. I'll see it through."

"What's your name, son?" another of the men asked.

"Joshua Sims, sir."

"You won't be coming back to town, Joshua. Will your folks allow you to stay away for such a long period of time?" this man asked.

"Don't have any folks. I'm on my own," he lied.

"Be here at noon today. If we get three more men, we'll be ready to roll. We'll just see if you're as dependable as you say."

The men turned back to their coffee, and Joshua raced back to the inn.

He went directly to his room and packed all his belongings. He wondered how he would break the news to Priscilla. He carried all he owned to the veranda and placed it behind a wicker rocker, sat down, and waited.

A short time later, Walter opened the picket gate for Priscilla and they joined him. Joshua had never seen Priscilla so excited.

"Mr. Nelson at the livery said that the mail coach will be here in a day or two, and we could exchange Daddy's harness-making equipment for passage all the way to Buffalo. And Mrs. Nelson is interested in Mother's quilt," she said breathlessly.

Joshua was shocked. Trade their parents' things to get to Buffalo? It seemed immoral.

"There's more. I described Mother's dulcimer. He thinks it will fetch a good price somewhere along the way. Enough for food and lodging for the entire trip!" Priscilla clasped her hands across her chest. "I am so relieved."

Priscilla dropped into the chair next to Joshua. "What have you been doing today?" she asked.

"Looking and lots of thinking," he said. "I'm not going to Buffalo."

"Of course, you're going to Buffalo."

"I have a job. I will make enough in one year to pay off the entire debt on the homestead," he announced.

"Have you gone daft?" Priscilla said. "What kind of job could *you* get?"

"I'm going to be a road builder. I'm on my way right now to catch a wagon to go to the job."

"You are not! We're going to Buffalo. It's all decided."

"I'm not going! And I'll run away if you try to force me into it," he said as he picked up his gear and stepped from the porch.

"Good luck, Priscilla. Walter, don't forget we're partners. I'll see you sooner than you think."

"You will die here," Priscilla warned bitterly. "And I hope you do!"

Joshua continued walking.

"You come back here," she shouted. "Walter, tell him to come back."

"He'll come back, Priscilla. He'll come back."

But he didn't go back. At noon he boarded the wagon with the other workers.

10

In a Trader's Cabin in Western Ohio

A familiar clicking sound jarred Sims from his slumber. It was a sound he had heard often when he went hunting with Daddy—the cocking of a flintlock. The first thing he saw through squinted eyes was the long barrel of a musket inches from his throat.

Above him loomed a very large man in a buffalo hide coat and hat. The man was of mixed parentage—Sims guessed French and Indian. The giant's massive arms protruded three inches beyond the sleeves of his ice-crusted coat. His high cheekbones and leathery olive skin hinted at his Indian heritage. His hat, cocked forward at a rakish angle, rested just above his scowling eyebrows. An ornate powder horn dangled from a cord around his neck.

"Well, M'sieur le Nu, do you tell me why you've broken into my house, or do I separate your head from your body?" the man said in a thick accent.

Sims's instant thought was that he had been mistaken for someone else—someone this giant obviously didn't like.

"My name is Sims. I had to get out of the storm and there wasn't anyone here. If you let me up, I'll get my clothes and leave."

Sims closed his eyes again, his every muscle tensed. He feared that his next breath would be his last. In that instant, he recalled what Mr. Johnson had said. "Never trust a half-breed. They can't decide what they are. They're Indian when it's to their advantage and white if that benefits them."

Sims couldn't speak.

Then, with a loud laugh that shook the room, the man withdrew his musket and said in a booming voice, "No telling who's going to turn up these days. All you settlers wandering around. Can't get away from 'em any more'n you can get away from the flies."

He leaned his musket against the wall. "Rémy Duval at your service. Call me Le Boeuf, like everyone else does."

Sims sighed as the blood returned to his face. "I just came here to get out of the storm. I meant no harm."

"Well, get your clothes on. I'll go get breakfast."

"I don't plan to stay. I'll just get my things and be on my way."

"Wherever you're going, you cannot get there. Do you have coffee?"

Sims nodded.

"I ran out days ago. You brew some, M'sieur le Nu, and I'll furnish the rest."

Le Boeuf flung the door open. In the early morning glare, Sims saw a wonderland of ice-covered snow. Trees bowed under the weight. Large limbs littered the ground, having been ripped from the trees by their burden of ice.

Le Boeuf grabbed a walking stick from the corner and bounded out the door. He nearly lost his footing on the slick ground. He steadied himself against the shack. Using the stick to break a path in the ice, he strode into the woods.

Sims closed the door and quickly dressed. He stoked the coals in the fire ring. He poured the last of his water supply into his flagon and set it in the fire.

Sims thought it best to humor this strange man, but he was eager to get out of there. He put his things in order, ready to leave at the first opportunity.

He studied Le Boeuf's flintlock. Its broken shadow on the uneven wall reminded him of that fateful day at the homestead. This musket was almost identical to Daddy's. It had the same curly maple stock and brass butt plate. It had the oversized trigger guard. Two fingers could be used to squeeze off a shot.

The coffee was boiling when his host burst back into the shack, carrying two rabbits. He replaced his walking stick by the door. Sims could not help noticing the blood and gray fur on it.

"Not my idea of elegant breakfast fare. But these critters were sitting in a hole out there, shivering, and I couldn't pass 'em up." The man laughed.

Sims marveled at how quickly and expertly the man cleaned the rabbits. Le Boeuf kicked the door open and flung the offal outside.

"Oh, there's nothing better than the aroma of freshly brewed coffee," Le Boeuf said. He skewered the rabbits and hung them over the fire. "Now, *parlez*, what brings you to my abode?"

"I'm on my way down the Maumee. A Mister Chapman said I could stay here."

"You met Johnny? Now there's a strange bird for you. Not like all the other intruders roaming around." He stoked the fire and tested the rabbit meat with his knife. Deciding it needed more cooking, he hunkered near the flame, rested his elbows on his knees and stared at Sims. The intensity of his eyes made Sims's flesh creep. There was silence.

"You didn't expect to have breakfast with a half-breed, did you?" Le Boeuf mocked.

Sims was taken aback by this straightforward remark.

"Fact is, I am not a half-breed. I am five-eighths Potawatomi."

"Five-eighths?"

"That's the way I figure it. My French great-grandfather married a Potawatomi princess. So it was my grandfather who was the half-breed. My grandmother was Potawatomi. That made my father three-fourths Indian. My mother was half French, half Potawatomi. Calculate that, M'sieur le Nu. Five-eighths, *n'est-ce pas?*"

Le Boeuf moved the rabbits still closer to the blaze, where they blackened almost immediately. He turned the sizzling carcasses momentarily, removed their charred fare, and hacked a piece off with his knife, still bloody from the cleaning. He handed a piece to Sims, who thought it was less than appetizing, but took it anyway.

"What do you do, M'sieur le Nu, that brings you to the Maumee in an ice storm?"

"I'm with the team that's building the Michigan Road in Indiana," Sims said proudly.

"*Mon dieu!* A road builder? I should have shot you when I had the chance. I hold you personally responsible for destroying my livelihood," he said in his booming voice.

"Me? What did I do?"

"Roads make it too easy for people to get here. When it was difficult to get around the wilderness, only strong-hearted, good people came. With roads, the lazy, good-for-nothing riffraff come in droves. The better the roads, the lower the quality of the travelers," he snorted.

"That's hardly my fault. You think I'm personally to blame?" Sims said defensively.

"There's enough blame to go around," Le Boeuf said in an angry voice.

"What do you mean by that?" Sims looked sideways at his belongings, planning to escape if it came to that.

"Good roads make it easy for people to get in—and out.

Mark my word, M'sieur le Nu, when the good roads come, they'll first be used to take my Indian cousins out."

"I met a man who said that canals will replace roads," Sims said, hoping to change the subject.

"Canals? Worse than roads! Let me tell you about canals. At least when people come by roads, they ride wagons and are dressed for work. On canals, they are dandies dressed in frock coats and stovepipe hats. The ladies wear fine dresses and carry parasols to protect their lovely white skin. Useless people! They're spectators along for the ride, looking for whatever they can steal for themselves."

"Why do you say that?"

"The entire history of this continent is that way. The three Ms fuel the whole thing." His voice was more agitated than ever. He jabbed his hunting knife forcibly into the dirt near the fire ring.

"Three Ms?" Sims moved closer to his gear.

"Missionaries, military, and money! My French ancestors sent missionaries, 'black coats,' who stupefied the Indians and exploited them in the fur trade. The British sent their military, but their diseases killed more Indians than their bullets. And then your American government sent money to the wilderness, making the Indians rely on allotments instead of their traditional ways of life. My family has been in the fur trade for four generations, but I'm the end of the line. The three Ms destroyed my fur trade and the dignity of the tribes."

"My friend, Mr. Johnson, says we have a God-given right to be here." Sims picked up another piece of rabbit.

Le Boeuf spat. "Your Mr. Johnson is a fool! I don't say my Indian ancestors were saints. No, sir! What the Potawatomi did to the Illinois braves, starving them to death, wasn't saintly. I tell you, there's enough blame to go around. But the tribes were once proud. The three Ms crushed that way of life. The old ways are gone. You will understand that some day."

Sims wiped his mouth on his sleeve. "I'd be glad to pay you for your hospitality." Sims stood and turned to pick up his belongings.

"*Mon dieu!* You Americans think you can buy even hospitality with money. Where do you think you're going?"

"I need to get to Fort Defiance, and I don't have much time. I must be walking every daylight hour."

"Fort Defiance? One more example of Yanquee arrogance. Mad Anthony Wayne built a fort where the Maumee and Auglaize rivers come together. He stood on a rock and said, 'I defy the English, the Indians and all the devils in Hell to take it.' So they named it Fort Defiance. But, M'sieur le Nu, he forgot about the wilderness. No one had to capture it. It fell down. There hasn't been a Fort Defiance for nearly twenty years."

"But surely there's a settlement," Sims insisted. "I'm supposed to report there." Sims loaded up and moved to the door.

"If you think you can walk there, *au revoir*, M'sieur le Nu!"

Sims pushed open the door and stepped outside. When he hit the ice, his feet slipped out from under him. He fell on his backside and slid down the slope. Try as he would, he could not stop himself. He plummeted toward the cliff that overhung the river.

Just when he thought he would shoot over the bank into the icy water, the snarling teeth of a large animal grabbed him by the collar. Sims could smell the creature's foul breath. The animal tugged and dragged him back toward the cabin.

Le Boeuf stood in the doorway, doubled in laughter at Sims's plight. The animal released its grip on Sims and leapt on Le Boeuf. The animal and the man wrestled on the ground.

Le Boeuf pushed the animal away and, still laughing wildly, shouted, "M'sieur le Nu, meet Chien, my dog. He thinks he's five-eighths wolf."

He lifted himself to one knee and said, "Down, Chien. You've played enough." The large black dog wagged its tail wildly and jumped to lick Le Boeuf's face.

Sims crawled back to the cabin.

"Didn't I tell you that you couldn't walk to Defiance today?" Le Boeuf gloated.

"But I have a schedule," Sims protested.

"At noon. We'll leave at noon."

"You think the ice will be gone by then?"

"No ice in the river. We will go in my boat," he said, as he roughly rubbed Chien's head.

Back inside, Le Boeuf stoked the fire and removed some tools, familiar to Sims, from his possibles bag. He placed an iron ladle in the fire and added some scraps of lead. Soon the lead was molten. They were going to make ammunition. Sims had done this many times.

While Chien slept by his side, Le Boeuf resumed his family story. Working as he talked, he poured the molten lead into a bullet mold, then opened the mold and dumped the hot ball onto a flat rock to cool. Sims picked up the cooled lead balls and, using a special tool, cut the sprue, or mold mark, and smoothed the finished ball.

Sims spent the rest of the morning listening to stories and making musket balls. Le Boeuf told how his French great-grandfather came to America and went to Lake Michigan to start the family fur trading business. It was Le Boeuf's grandfather's exploits during the Seven Years' War that most interested Sims, however. The grandfather was a soldier for France who was garrisoned at Fort Duquesne in Pennsylvania. Sims remembered his teacher in Virginia telling about the war that he called the French and Indian War. His hero George Washington had fought in it. Sims was surprised to learn that they were the same war. Le Boeuf's version was not at all like his teacher's story.

"My father fought in the War of 1812," Le Boeuf said, dumping another ball from the mold. "This time on the

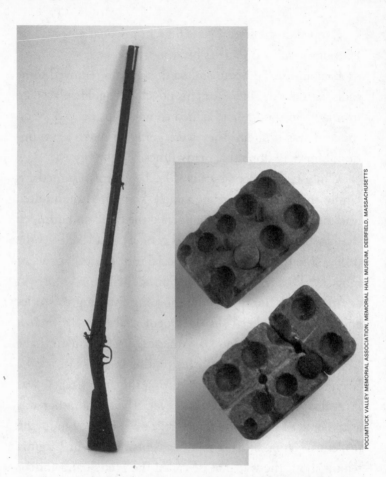

The flintlock muskets owned by Sims's father and by Le Boeuf would have looked similar to this musket, owned by John T. Graves, a soldier from Greenfield, Massachusetts. The mold that Sims and Le Boeuf used for making bullets may have looked similar to the soapstone bullet mold shown here. The musket and the mold are features of the Memorial Hall Museum, online at http://www.old-deerfield.org/.

side of the British. It's difficult to know whose side to be on if you're three-fourths Indian. Especially when both sides have betrayed you sometime or another."

As promised, they left for the river at noon. The ice had thawed, but it was still difficult to stand up. The brightness of the morning was gone. Now the sky was gray, and a chilling wind came out of the west.

The boat was hewn from a single log. Sims remembered from the stories that morning how Le Boeuf had helped his father make it. It was low in the back but swooped up in front. It was much longer and narrower than boats Sims had seen before. The middle of the boat was filled with trade goods, covered with a buffalo robe. Chien immediately jumped onto the robe and wagged his tail, anxious to begin the journey.

Le Boeuf reached under the buffalo robe and withdrew a pair of woolen mittens and threw them to Sims. He nodded and put them on immediately. He had seen mittens like this before. They had a flap in the palm so that the fingers could be exposed without removing the mittens, very handy if you needed bare fingers for such things as pulling the trigger on your gun.

"You ride in front, M'sieur le Nu," Le Boeuf said as he held the boat.

Sims stepped from the bank into the narrow boat. It swayed and turned violently.

"Asseyez-vous!" Le Boeuf shouted. "Sit down. Sit down."

To get his balance, Sims stepped into the knee-deep cold water. Chien barked and scolded him. Sims settled in the bow. After this false start, Le Boeuf shoved off, and they started downstream.

Sims had never rowed a canoe. His only instruction from Le Boeuf was, "Put your back into it, M'sieur le Nu." As talkative as Le Boeuf was ashore, he was equally silent on the water.

Sims immediately felt the cold through his wet trousers. His legs soon cramped. The energy he used paddling warmed his upper body, but his feet were freezing. The pain in his legs intensified, and the relentless wind sweeping across the water chilled him to the bone. Finally, he unwrapped his blanket and threw it around his legs.

Chien kept a constant vigil of the shoreline. A few hours into their journey, the black dog perked his ears, sat on his haunches and began to bark excitedly. Le Boeuf steered the boat to shore.

In moments, two Indians, an old man and a young boy, emerged from the brush carrying a small bundle of furs. Le Boeuf greeted them. They spoke in a language of their own, a mixture of French, English, and some native tongue.

Sims understood little of the transaction. He did understand when Le Boeuf repeated several times, "Pony, you know you don't get whiskey from me."

Finally they agreed on a trade. Le Boeuf handed the old man some of the musket balls they had made that morning. He called to Sims. "Catch, M'sieur le Nu."

Sims wondered why the Indians laughed.

Le Boeuf threw the bundle of furs to Sims. They turned and started to leave.

"Eat well, Ox," the old Indian said. "You too, Mr. Naked." The two Indians disappeared, laughing as they walked away.

Mr. Naked? Sims thought. He said to Le Boeuf, "Why did that man call me Mr. Naked? Is that what you've been calling me?"

"A fitting name, don't you think? You have to admit that when I first saw you, you weren't exactly dressed to entertain polite company. *Nous allons.* Let's go."

"My name is Sims," he protested. "Joshua Sims."

Sims intended to leave Le Boeuf at Fort Defiance. Instead, they went by canoe all the way to Perrysburg. At each place where they stopped to trade, they were Ox and Mr. Naked.

11

Sims had been sitting on the busy dock by Lake Erie for hours. The somber November sky reflected his mood. His clothes were in tatters. His hands, blistered from rowing, throbbed. But the battle raging in his mind was more painful than his aching muscles.

The thought of going to Buffalo instead of Detroit had haunted him since Jonathan Chapman had told him about the quarantine of Detroit. It came back more and more as he suffered the misery of rowing the canoe to Perrysburg. Now the notion made him smile. He pictured Mr. Johnson tracking him as far as Port Lawrence, only to find that he had vanished.

To do this would mean deserting his road-building job and losing a half-year of pay. It was contrary to his upbringing. "If you say you're going to do something, do it!" Daddy used to say.

Still, he had sent sixty dollars of his earnings with Ansel Kelly to the land office in Logansport. That had paid the next installment on the homestead. Walter had surely paid the rest. The homestead was almost certainly theirs by now. He had taken the job to keep his promise. Now the job seemed less important. He had thought of this before, and each time he'd say under his breath, "And you thought I couldn't do it, Priscilla. Ha-ha and so there!"

He could go to Buffalo and be back at the homestead in time for spring planting. He tapped the money pouch next to his chest.

He watched passengers and freight being loaded on a schooner bound for Buffalo, New York. He yearned to buy a ticket.

He had learned in Perrysburg that the quarantine of Detroit had been lifted. This news had not found its way into the frontier. So he could go there after all and finish the trip. That's what Daddy would have done.

He had also found out about Port Lawrence when he reported to his checkpoint. Some businessmen from Cincinnati had developed it, expecting to use their profits to invest in canals. It had quickly become a commercial center. He was told that federal wagons came there every day or so, and he could easily catch a supply wagon all the way to Detroit. He was still seventy miles from Detroit and two days behind schedule.

As he hunkered on the dock, Sims played over and over in his head all the experiences of his ten days with Le Boeuf. He had seen firsthand the hard life of the Indians along the Maumee River.

With each settler who had moved in, the Indians' lives had become harder. The fragile swamp environment was stretched beyond its limit. Deer had once been plentiful, but now with settlers and Indians hunting them, they had all but disappeared. Many of the fishing streams were polluted from the runoff produced by clearing trees to farm forested land. But the Indians, as poor as they were, had welcomed Le Boeuf and Sims into their villages.

Sims and Le Boeuf had to portage where the rapids extended the full width of the river. The weather was cold and miserable, and they were soaked up to their waists.

They tied the canoe on the south bank of the river. Sims hoped they would stay at an inn, so they could dry out in warm surroundings. But instead of going to the nearby village of Gilead, Le Boeuf had led him from rock to rock across the river.

"People have been crossing the river here for thousands of years," Le Boeuf had said. "It's the only way to get across for miles."

Le Boeuf took him to a small Indian village where they were greeted by some of Le Boeuf's friends. They were treated to a grand meal and invited to stay there for the night. At first, Sims was uneasy about the accommodations. But once inside the domed house made of cattail stems, with its surprisingly light interior, the soothing aroma of sweetgrass, and cozy warmth from the tiny fire in the middle, he dried off and had the best night's sleep since he left the homestead.

Sims compared that night with one two nights later when they stayed at a Presbyterian mission. There they had

PHOTO BY ELIZABETH BIRKY, COURTESY OF HISTORIC SAUDER VILLAGE, ARCHBOLD, OHIO,
HTTP://WWW.SAUDERVILLAGE.ORG)

Native Americans who lived near waterways, such as the Great Lakes and major rivers, often built houses out of the materials they found in the marshes. Cattails would have been used in areas where they were abundant. The wigwams shown here are re-creations at Historic Sauder Village—near where Sims enjoyed a cozy night of sleep among his native hosts, along the Maumee River.

slept in a log house that was so breezy he nearly froze. In addition, four other men had occupied the room he stayed in. There was just one bed, so they all lay across it like cordwood. Two of his bedfellows snored so loudly that it fairly shook the walls; another passed gas all night. Le Boeuf had wisely decided to stay in the woodshed with his dog that night.

Along the way, he had carried furs and transferred trade goods from the place of trading to the canoe. Sometimes it was difficult work to scramble down the slippery riverbank and secure the furs in the canoe. In Sims's mind, at least, the work he did balanced out. It was his way of being true to his father's saying. He did not want to be beholden to Le Boeuf.

Time and time again he had seen Le Boeuf give the Indians trade goods worth more than the furs. Then he gave them money if their allotments were used up. There were frequent requests for liquor as a condition of barter. Le Boeuf refused each time. Sims had soon realized that Le Boeuf was no ordinary trader.

The day before they reached Perrysburg was one he would never forget. They were close to the site of the Battle of Fallen Timbers. It was a place Sims had learned about in school. His teacher back in Virginia said that this was the battle that opened up the western territory for settlement.

In Le Boeuf's version, it was the beginning of the end for everything he knew and cherished.

"Chief Turkeyfoot stood there on a rock," he had said, pointing north. "He rallied his warriors and made one final charge against the troops. They were outnumbered, wounded, and exhausted. It was courageous, but disastrous." His voice had wavered with emotion, and tears had welled up in the eyes of this huge, tough man. No, Sims could never forget that.

Sims waited on the dock, but he was unsure what he waited for, a wagon to Detroit or a boat to Buffalo. He unfolded his map for the fourth time. Le Boeuf had drawn an additional line on it with charcoal when Sims told him about his schedule.

"The Sauk Trail is north of the swamp. It would be a quicker way back. By the time you head south, the swamp will be frozen. It would save you about five days," Le Boeuf had said.

Le Boeuf's suggestion appealed to him, even though it was against orders. The idea of following the Maumee back to Fort Wayne without Le Boeuf worried him, now that he knew how dangerous the terrain was.

By dusk, the crowd on the dock had thinned out. There were no more boats going to Buffalo, and no supply wagon had shown up that would take him to Detroit. He absentmindedly scratched two arrows into the sand. One pointed east toward Buffalo, the other pointed north toward Detroit.

He folded his map quickly. He had made his decision. Whichever came first, a boat to Buffalo or a wagon to Detroit. He would let fate decide his future.

A small sailboat docked near where he had squatted all day. On the bow, painted in large red letters, was its name, *Phoebus*. A middle-aged man in fine clothes talked briefly to the captain, then turned and hurried past Sims to a waiting carriage. He returned with a stylishly dressed woman holding the hand of a small child. Behind her was a black woman servant, also well-dressed and carrying a baby. Following her, a young black girl in a checkered scarf and a fur-collared coat carried two carpetbags. At the end of the procession, an elderly black man pushed a steamer trunk on a cart.

When they filed past Sims, his heart skipped a beat. The black servants were the girl, her mother, and the old man—three of the runaways he had met before.

The girl in the scarf recognized Sims, but instantly the eyes that had shone so brightly in the forest clouded with fear. She looked at Sims and shook her head, then quickened her step.

They waited briefly behind a loaded wagon until they were sure no one was watching. Then all of them except the girl quickly boarded the *Phoebus*. A sailor hustled them below deck. The girl ran back and stood for a moment looking past Sims.

"Sims?" she whispered.

He nodded.

"We have to be very careful. Two men are looking for us."

"I saw them," Sims whispered.

"Here?" she said in a voice filled with panic.

"No, in Fort Wayne." Sims studied the small crowd on the dock, searching for the roughnecks who had threatened him. "I don't see them here."

"We're pretending to be the servants of our white friends. We're taking a boat to Detroit."

"Detroit?"

She nodded and glanced furtively around the small crowd. "I have to go," she said.

She ran to the carriage, picked up a small scarf and scampered back, boarded the boat, and disappeared below.

What a remarkable coincidence, Sims thought. He never supposed he would see the travelers again, but here they were. Then it hit him. He had been waiting for either a boat to Buffalo or a wagon to Detroit. Here was a boat to Detroit.

He ran his hand deep into his shoulder bag. He pulled out the voucher Captain Brown had given him.

He approached the boat's captain. "You're going to Detroit?" Sims asked.

"We might be," he said.

"I'd like to go with you."

The captain's eyes narrowed. He looked Sims over from head to toe.

"We don't carry passengers. We're a cargo ship," the captain said in a coarse voice.

Sims was perplexed. He had just seen passengers board.

"Could I get passage with this voucher?" He handed the document to the captain.

As soon as the captain saw the official seal on the voucher, his manner changed. "You certainly can, young man, if you don't mind riding with the rest of the cargo. We do a lot of shipping for the federal government."

"How long will it take to get to Detroit?"

"With good wind, we should be there tomorrow," the captain said. He turned to sign a bill of lading for a man loading some crates of chickens.

Sims had expected it to take four days to get from Port Lawrence to Detroit. He had lost a day waiting for a wagon. He saw his chance to make up some time.

Sims boarded the vessel and waited at the railing. The captain joined him as the last rays of the sun reflected in the lake. The instant before a sailor cast off the ropes, the stylish couple and their two children leaped ashore. They were carrying the clothes the former slaves had worn.

"Now," the captain said to Sims, "Let me see that voucher again. I have to be very careful of the cargo I carry. But I never heard of a bounty hunter carrying a survey voucher." After the captain copied some information from the voucher, he added, "You can go below with the cargo."

When Sims arrived below deck, the girl said, "You scared me when I saw you, Sims. I thought that you were looking for us after all."

"I was surprised to see you, too. Where's the rest of the group you were traveling with?"

"Samuel has gone back south, and…."

"Sarah, don't burden him with your talk," her mother said in a stern voice.

A sailor brought soup and dried bread. They ate in silence, then Sims went on deck to breathe the night air.

ASHTABULA HARBOR, CA. 1855–1920, AL03153, WILBUR H. SIEBERT COLLECTION, MSS 116 AV, OHIO HISTORICAL SOCIETY

Pictured here is Ashtabula Harbor, along Lake Erie in northeastern Ohio. The photograph shows one of many harbors where fugitive slaves boarded boats that took them across Lake Erie to safety and freedom in Canada. Port Lawrence, where Toledo sits on Lake Erie today, would have been a safe harbor for fugitive slaves as well.

The moon had been full two nights before he left the base camp. Now the night was black. Even stars could not penetrate the darkness. The sails strained against the mast in the brisk wind. The only sounds were the flutter of the sails, the lake water lapping against the boat, and an occasional mournful bleat of a horn from a nearby ship.

As the captain promised, they arrived at the Detroit harbor on the second dark night. A sailor jumped to the deserted dock and tied off the craft. He swung an oil lantern in a sweeping motion, set it on the dock, and leapt back aboard.

Within minutes, a wagon pulled up to the dock. The travelers jumped ashore and ran to the wagon. Even in the dim lantern light, Sims could tell that this was no ordinary farm wagon. He could clearly see that under the load of hay there was a secret compartment.

Sarah helped the old man scoot into this cramped space. Then her mother lifted their belongings into the wagon and climbed in.

The girl turned and waved. "God be with you, Sims," she said as she jumped into the wagon. The driver quickly rearranged the hay to conceal the runaways, jumped to the buck seat, slapped the horses with the lines, and clattered away into the night.

Sims watched until the wagon was gone. He sat down on the railing and said under his breath, "God be with you, too, Sarah."

Sims stayed aboard the *Phoebus* until morning. The captain gave him directions to the federal land office. He was sitting on the steps there as the workers arrived and immediately presented the order for ink to a clerk.

The white-haired clerk wore a leather visor. He rolled up his shirt sleeves and studied the order.

"Ink?" the man said. "We don't have that much. I'll see what I can do."

The man left his desk and returned a few minutes later with a packet wrapped in waxed sailcloth. "There are only a few papers of ink in here, but it's as much as I can spare. It should get you through until spring."

It took Sims several minutes to figure out a way to lash the square parcel. It was too large to go into either of his shoulder bags. He finally untied his blanket and used the leather thongs to attach the package to his belt. He draped his blanket over his shoulders. It was awkward, but he managed.

"I was ordered to return to the Michigan Road survey camp the way I came," he said to the clerk. "I've been studying my map, and I think it would be quicker to go back by way of the Sauk Trail."

He shoved his map across the counter and pointed at the charcoal line that Le Boeuf had drawn. The clerk slid his spectacles to the end of his bulbous nose. "Where was the end of the road when you left?"

Sims pointed to the map northwest of Tiptonville.

"It's a nasty trip either way. Take the Sauk Trail, and you end up about fifty miles from the road."

"But they've built the road north while I've been gone," Sims pointed out.

"True enough. But there won't be many white settlements that way. You could get lost. Besides, that takes you through Potawatomi country. They're a little upset since the Chicago Treaty."

Sims thought of Le Boeuf. Having known someone who was five-eighths Potawatomi had lessened the fear of Indians he had when he started his trek.

"I'm going to chance it," Sims said in a confident voice. "If I get lost, I'd rather be there than in the swamps along the Maumee."

"There won't be any checkpoints," the clerk warned.

"I heard the Sauk Trail would save me five days, and I'm behind schedule. Mr. Johnson would be mad if I was late and he had already started looking for me before I got back. I'd have to go looking for him."

"I'm glad you're doing it and not me. The Sauk Trail is more direct, though."

"That settles it. If anyone comes looking for Joshua Sims, tell them that's the way I went."

The clerk told Sims how to get to the head of the trail.

"Good luck," the man said.

By nightfall, Sims was well west of Detroit, walking his measured step, counting, and checking his compass every three miles.

12

On the Sauk Trail in Southern Michigan

The wind had shifted and was coming from the northeast. It brought with it a bitter chill from Lake Erie. Frequent drizzle found every hole in Sims's clothes. The days of wading in the Maumee had demolished his shoes. Now his left boot had pulled apart at the sole, exposing his bare foot through a hole in his sock.

Still, he made good progress. The trail was easy to follow, and it was solid ground, unlike the land where he started or that around much of the Maumee. Although Sims had to cross several rivers and streams, none were as large as the Maumee. Along the Sauk Trail, none had steep banks like the Maumee featured in places either.

Now that a sliver of moon grew in the nighttime sky, Sims felt comfortable extending his walking hours into darkness. He was certain that he could cover twenty miles a day if the weather held. He increased his pace.

As Sims walked, he congratulated himself on his decision to finish the job. The promise of receiving a bonus gave him a new image of the homestead. He'd buy a team of fine draft horses, a wagon, and a plow designed especially for turning the prairie soil. He'd have a proper house and barn. When this was accomplished, then he'd go to Buffalo.

But the weather didn't hold. On his second day, the sky darkened, and snow clouds swept the horizon. Sims had slept in the open alongside the trail the night before. If snow came tonight, he would have to find shelter. Furthermore, he was almost out of food again. By the time the snow started falling, he had little left except some pemmican and coffee.

That night, after the snow began, Sims constructed a lean-to from small branches. He built his fire close to the entrance, hoping that the heat would warm the space and the bright light would scare away the wolves he had been hearing in the distance. During the night he awoke with a hacking cough.

The next day, Sims struggled through a sheet of snow driven by a frightful wind. By noon of that day, his head hurt, and his ears burned. He put his hands under his chin. No question about it—fever.

By evening Sims had stumbled into a depression beside the trail. The wind was freezing. His muscles ached, and his forehead dripped with sweat. During the night, Sims awoke from a nightmare in which he and Miller searched a swamp looking in vain for Mr. Johnson.

The next morning Sims tried twice to get out from under his ice-encrusted blanket.

"I've got to get up. Miller says that you know you're freezing to death if all you want to do is sleep," he said. Then Sims realized that he was talking aloud. On the third try, he stood. Walking in the freezing snow had finished the job on his left boot. He stopped within the first mile to discard it. Sims cut a strip from his blanket and wrapped his foot, tying the swath in place with his shoestring.

Sims did not eat that day, but he walked. How he was able to keep walking, he didn't know. By midday, his chest began to hurt, and he was spitting phlegm that froze before it hit the ground. His nightmares of being chased by wolves, unable to run, invaded his waking hours. These hallucinations became so vivid that when they left, Sims found himself running wildly and shouting obscenities at imaginary wolves.

Then came the humming in his ears, the tingling of every nerve in his body. Sims fell.

Sims awoke in a bed in a tiny log cabin. A fire roared in the hearth. A young man, dressed in a black coat and a ruffled shirt, held a steaming bowl of stew above him.

"Decided to come back, I see," the young man said.

Sims looked at him through bleary eyes.

"You're a lucky one," the man said. He filled a ladle and held it for Sims to sip.

"Where am I?" Sims croaked in confusion.

"You're safe. If I hadn't found you when I did, you would be dead now. Here, get some of this in your belly."

The warmth of the stew soothed Sims's sore throat. Soon his eyes began to focus. Finally, he got a good look at the man who had saved him from the storm. He had Indian features, but his dress was certainly American. His hair was neatly trimmed and his hands were not those of a working man. He was slender, not much taller than Sims.

"How do you feel now?"

"My chest really hurts," Sims said, as a violent chill made him shudder.

"I can hear that your throat must be hurting as well. When you finish eating, I'll give you some medicine."

He handed Sims the bowl and brought a leather case to his bedside. For the first time Sims surveyed his surroundings. The cabin was small, with the usual frontier furniture. The big difference was the bookshelf above the small desk. On the frontier books were so rare that he had to look twice to believe what he was seeing. On either side of the desk hung drawings of the human anatomy.

"I'm Luther," the man said as he opened a black leather bag. "Who are you?"

"Joshua Sims," he said in a voice that was barely audible. Sims could see that the bag contained several glass bottles.

"I'll have you feeling better in no time at all."

"You a doctor?"

"I studied medicine at the mission school. Let me see your tongue."

Sims opened his mouth and stuck out his tongue. Luther looked at it, pulled down Sims's eyelids, and squinted at each eye. Then he poured powder from two bottles into a mortar and ground it with a pestle to pulverize the mixture. He added a small amount of water to make a paste, then rolled it out into several perfect pills.

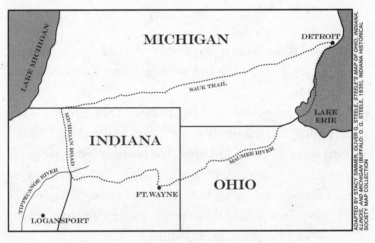

This map shows the approximate route of Sims's journey, which began in Indiana (bottom left) at Tiptonville near where the Tippecanoe River crosses Michigan Road, went through Fort Wayne, northeastern Ohio (bottom right), Lake Erie (far right), Detroit (top right corner), along the Sauk Trail in southern Michigan (top), and back near Tiptonville.

Sims swallowed two of the pills and lay back on the soft pillow. He hadn't slept on a real pillow since he left his family's homestead more than a year ago. It's hard to say whether it was the warmth of the fire, the stomach full of stew, or the medicine, but he dropped into a deep sleep.

When he stirred the next morning, Luther asked, "Well, how do you feel this day?"

"Better," Sims said in a raspy voice that hurt his throat.

"You had a good sleep. Are you hungry?"

Sims nodded.

"Can you get up?"

"I think so." He sat on the edge of the bed.

"Come to the table and we'll get some warm food into your body."

His knees were weak. He wobbled to the table.

Luther had prepared a meal of cornbread and beans. Sims had not eaten anything that tasted so good since his mother died. *Since Mother died*, he thought. A twinge of grief flitted through his hazy mind. A fleeting image of the pile of rocks where both his parents lay melted into a sigh.

"What brings you here, Joshua?"

"I had to go to Detroit to get ink for the Michigan Road-building crew. I'm on my way back now. I have to be home in just a few days."

"You went all the way to Detroit to get ink? The makings for ink were all around you. My people have been making pigments for centuries."

Sims felt the heat of embarrassment.

Luther sensed his uneasiness. "Well, we all do what we're told whether it makes sense or not. You must be very dependable to make such a difficult trip." He turned to look at Sims's gear in a pile on the floor. "So it's ink in that packet. I wondered what it was."

Sims nodded and stroked his sore throat.

"You need to rest today. We must leave tomorrow. I'll make sure you get on the right trail."

Sims finished his meal, took two more of Luther's pills, and went to bed. He fell immediately into a deep slumber.

It was morning before Sims roused from his sleep. He felt much better, but he was still lightheaded.

Luther was not in the house. Sims stepped outside and saw him, shirtless, sitting on a knoll a short distance from the house. Sims stepped back into the doorway and watched.

Luther sat as if in a trance. At intervals, he removed more of his clothing until he sat totally naked in the cold air. Then, just as ceremoniously, he put on his Potawatomi garments. He pulled on loose-fitting breeches, a buckskin shirt, and a waistcoat. He wrapped a beaded sash around his middle, draped a colorful blanket across his shoulder, and put on a turban-like headdress with an orange streamer down the back. He sat again to put his feet into beaded deerskin boots. Then he stood, picked up the neatly folded pile of American clothes, and headed toward the cabin.

Sims moved back toward the table and waited. Luther came in and placed the pile of clothes on the table in front of him.

"Your clothes are worn out. Dress in these. We will leave after you eat," Luther said. His voice was calm, yet distant. His manner had changed.

Luther said nothing more. Sims did as he was told. In a moment, he was transformed from a ragged frontiersman into a finely dressed gentleman, with riding boots, ruffled shirt and shoestring tie, vest, woolen scarf, beaver hat, and full-length coat.

Sims ate cornbread and jerky. Luther did not.

Sims picked up his shoulder bags and the precious packet of ink. They went outside.

Two horses were tied at the back of the cabin. The paint had a fine saddle. Sims's experience with harnesses told him that it was very expensive indeed. Two bulging bags hung from the saddle horn.

In contrast the bay was draped only with an Indian blanket and a bedroll.

"You ride the paint," Luther said. "He will carry you to your destination in good order."

Sims was perplexed, but said nothing.

Luther tapped the cloth bags strapped to the saddle. "Food and medicine for you in this one—sweet feed for the horse in this one. Mount up," Luther said.

They rode several yards from the cabin.

"Hold my horse," Luther said.

Luther sprang to the ground. He stood silently for a long moment with his hands on his hips and stared at the cabin.

Then he went back inside. Minutes passed. Sims smelled smoke and thought that Luther had quenched the fire in the fireplace. Suddenly, he emerged carrying a small bundle wrapped in a beaded banner. Through the open door Sims could see that the entire inside of the house was ablaze.

Sims shouted, "Your house is on fire!" He started to dismount, but Luther held up his hand.

"Potawatomi means 'people of the fire,'" he said simply. He mounted his horse and without looking back, said, "It's time to leave."

They rode west on the Sauk Trail all morning. Sims had no idea what was happening. All he could think of was the cozy cabin where this young doctor had nursed him. He could still see the shelf of precious books, books that by now were cinders.

Just as Sims heard the distant sound of horses ahead, they turned on to a small trail that meandered to the south. They rode a few yards, then Luther stopped. He jumped from his horse and motioned for Sims to dismount.

"You must be wondering what's going on. This morning I cleansed myself of white men's ways. Today I am Wap-kizhett—White Pigeon."

"What do you mean?" Sims asked.

"You eat. I must fast." His voice was relaxed, like some-one who had been relieved of a great burden.

Sims was hungry. He reached into the saddlebag and withdrew a chunk of cornbread.

"A few months ago, several Potawatomi chiefs signed a treaty in Chicago. They had no right to speak for all Potawatomi. It wasn't a treaty. It was treason."

As Wapkizhett spoke, the noise Sims had heard earlier became louder, and he saw a line of Indians traveling east on the Sauk Trail. At first it was just a few Indians, then more and more.

"The agreement these treasonous chiefs made destroyed the Potawatomi nation. All our land and other holdings are gone."

As Sims listened, he watched the eerie procession on the trail.

"Those of us who are angry at these chiefs have denounced the white man's way of life. We have gone back to our traditional ways. We will not live here under this treaty. We are going to Canada."

The trail was now filled with people, some riding and some walking.

"I will leave you here. Three days on this trail will bring you to Chief Menominee's town," he said. "I judge you to be very trustworthy and dependable. Anyone who would journey so far for ink must be dependable."

Wapkizhett handed Sims the beaded parcel he had carried all morning. "Give this to Menominee in person. Tell him that Wapkizhett sent it. He will know the rest."

Sims took the parcel, his face filled with astonishment.

"It's time for me to go with my people, Joshua."

"What will I do with your horse?"

"Leave it with my people in Menominee's town."

"How do I repay you for all you've done? You saved my life. I don't know what to say," Sims said. His voice trembled with helplessness.

"Say nothing. Just deliver the packet. Don't let me down. That will be payment enough," Wapkizhett said. With that, he sprung to his mount and galloped back to join the caravan of his people.

Sims stood looking in amazement as Wapkizhett disappeared. What a story he would have to tell Miller when he got back!

The last leg of his journey turned out to be the easiest. He had a good horse, food, and warm clothing. He followed the trail that meandered on the high ground through the swamp. Le Boeuf was right: it was frozen and not as hazardous as it had been when he left nearly a month ago.

Just as Wapkizhett predicted, Sims arrived at Chief Menominee's town in three days. He asked to see Menominee in person and was taken to his house. The town of Menominee was larger than other Indian towns he had seen during his travels, with even more people than Logansport, he guessed. There were several log homes, but most of the people lived in cattail houses.

Sims was shocked when he met Chief Menominee. He knew this man! He had seen him at the Chippeway treaty grounds and many times at Tiptonville. Those times, the mere sight of the man had caused instant terror. Now there was no such emotion.

"Wapkizhett asked me to deliver this to you in person," Sims said to Menominee as he handed the parcel to the chief.

"This is a priceless treasure," Menominee said, accepting it. "It is the sacred bundle of Wapkizhett's clan. He sent it as a reminder to sell no more land to the white man." He cradled the bundle in his hands almost reverently. "And Wapkizhett? He is well?"

"Yes. Wapkizhett saved my life. I owe him very much, and I don't know how to repay him," Sims said.

He knew that he would always be beholden to Wapkizhett—and to Samuel and Sarah, the McDermotts, Chief Richardville, Jonathan Chapman, and Le Boeuf. How could he ever be true to his father's words again?

"You have repaid Wapkizhett fully by bringing this to me. Will you stay as my guest for a while?"

"I'm much obliged for the offer, sir. But I need to be on my way. It's still a long walk to the base camp."

"Take Wapkizhett's horse. You have earned it."

It was the morning of the second day after he left Chief Menominee when Sims rode into the base camp, two full days ahead of schedule. He saw Miller tying his team outside the cook tent. He nudged his horse and reined in beside him.

This stone monument of Chief Menominee is located in Marshall County, Indiana, near the site of Menominee's town, about halfway between South Bend and Tiptonville. The memorial was erected in 1909 to commemorate the removal of Menominee and his band of Potawatomi Indians in 1838.

"Yo, Miller," he shouted, as he grabbed the sailcloth packet from the saddle and jumped down.

"Sims? Is that you, Sims?" Miller asked in disbelief.

"True enough."

"Sims, you left here looking like a ragamuffin, and you come back on a fine horse, looking like a circuit judge. How can this be true?"

"You won't believe it," Sims grinned.

Miller gave Sims a boyish punch on the arm. They followed the aroma of sizzling sausage and flapjacks into the cook tent.

"What's in the package?" Miller asked.

Sims smiled.

"Ink."

Afterword

What is the real story of the trek to Detroit to get ink? No one knows. All the things that happened to Sims, a fictitious character, could have happened to a person who actually made this journey. There are people in northern Indiana who believe the trip did take place and that a boy named Hobbs did it in the allotted time. A South Bend newspaper article mentions the journal entry at the beginning of this story, and a Fulton County conservation officer mentions the journal entry in talks that he gives to the public. However, exhaustive research by the author failed to uncover any additional information on Hobbs or the trip.

In telling the fictional story of Joshua Sims's travels from the area around what is now Rochester, Indiana, to Detroit, Michigan, and back, many fictional figures were created. However, the story is also peopled with actual historic figures, who left their marks on the vanishing frontier in remarkable ways. For example, Levi Coffin is important to the story of the Underground Railroad;

Born in Tennessee in 1786, John Tipton settled in Indiana Territory by 1804. At first he was a farmer and a militiaman. Later he entered politics, serving as an Indiana State Representative and then as a United States Senator. He also served as an Indian agent. Similar to Tiptonville, Tipton, Indiana, and Tipton County, Indiana, are both named for John Tipton.

Jonathan Chapman became the legendary Johnny Appleseed; and Chief Menominee and his band were forcibly removed from Indiana in 1838.

The frontier was truly a place of great activity involving many different people moving across the wilderness for many different reasons. If a real boy Hobbs actually undertook the journey to Detroit, he would have encountered a lot of the same people in the same circumstances that Sims encountered in this fictional story.

The hardships the Sims family endured were not uncommon. The reason for their immigration—cheap land—and the modes of transportation they used—flatboat, ox and cart—are authentic. Unscrupulous land speculators or their agents often took advantage of settlers and the native population. Disease, accidents, and hardships were a constant part of a fragile existence on the frontier.

Occasional hostilities between Native Americans and pioneers was also a reality, with individuals on both sides attacking and murdering peaceful people from the other group. For this reason, states employed militias to keep order. The fictitious Captain Eli Turner and his unit of soldiers represent this portion of the early Indiana landscape.

The Irishman Mr. McDermott, another fictitious character, was wrong about the importance of the canals on the frontier. It is true that many were built. In fact, the Wabash and Erie Canal was the longest in the country. However, in the end, the canal system nearly bankrupted the state of Indiana, and railroads replaced most of the canals soon after they were built.

One of the most popular routes taken by runaway slaves went through the area where Sims traveled. Levi Coffin and his wife were but two of many early Hoosiers who helped these desperate people by hiding them; providing them with food, shelter, and clothing; and helping them to move from place to place. Many boats like the *Phoebus*, which traveled across the Great Lakes for business purposes, also smuggled "travelers" on the last leg of their journey into Canada and freedom. The many paths the travelers used and the many people who helped them have come to be known as the Underground Railroad.

While Le Boeuf is a fictional character, his situation and insight were a real part of the tapestry of the times. In the years after Sims's adventure, Le Boeuf's prophecies became reality. The last treaty ceding the remaining Native American land was signed, and the official enforced removal of the Native Americans in northern Indiana began. The historical General John Tipton came home to supervise the exodus to the Indiana state line. Judge William Polke, the same Polke whose inn Sims slept near the first night of his journey, was appointed to supervise the removal west from Illinois to Kansas.

Approximately fifty Native Americans died on this "Trail of Death," made by Chief Menominee and nearly eight hundred Potawatomi in 1838. More than half of those who died were children. In fact, the first child died no more than thirty miles from the start, near the location of the fictional Adam Miller's accident with the chain. A small monument south of Rochester marks the spot. The removal of these people is remembered each year in Rochester, where, in a two-day event called "Trail of Courage," parts of that tragic journey are reenacted.

The real boy named Hobbs, known as Joshua Sims in this book, could have lived to see the decline of the canal system in Indiana. This photograph, taken in 1898, when he would have been around 78 years old, shows the remains of part of the Wabash and Erie Canal near Fort Wayne.

The character of Mr. Johnson exemplifies prevailing American attitudes of the time about African Americans, Native Americans, and new immigrants such as the Irish. While we look upon his prejudices today with horror, those people who held the same views back in the pioneer era did not realize how inhumane they were. Prejudice can cover up a lot of conscience. It is only because we see the bigotry after nearly two centuries of experience that we recognize the ugliness of it.

Before we become too critical of Mr. Johnson, it would be wise to evaluate our own bigotry. What beliefs do we secretly harbor today that are every bit as unfeeling and inhumane as his? It is something to think about.

Glossary

Here are some words and terms that you may not know that you will find in the story of Joshua Sims. If there are other words in this story that you do not know, use your dictionary to learn what they mean.

allotment: An allowance.
awl: A tool used for punching holes in or sewing heavy material, such as leather.
ball: Ammunition in a round shape.
barter: Trade.
Battle of Fallen Timbers: The Battle of Fallen Timbers occurred on August 20, 1794, near where Toledo, Ohio, is today. General "Mad" Anthony Wayne and his American army fought and won the battle against a coalition of Indians including Delaware, Miami, Potawatomi, Shawnee, and several other tribes. After losing the battle, the Indians ceded most of Ohio to the United States by signing the Treaty of Greenville.
bay: A horse that is reddish-brown in color, with black mane, tail, and lower legs.

bedroll: A portable roll of bedding, usually one blanket tightly rolled and tied together with string or other fastening.

bill of lading: A document that notes the receipt of items for shipping.

blaze: A mark made to indicate the direction of a trail, often placed on trees.

blotter paper: A piece of paper used to absorb excess ink from a page.

bog: A type of wetland in which the ground is very soft and unstable.

bounty hunter: A person who catches fugitives for a monetary reward ("bounty"). During Sims's time, bounty hunters who searched for runaway slaves often were referred to as slave catchers.

brogue: An Irish accent.

buckshot: Large balls of lead used as ammunition.

burr: A plant seed that is covered in small hooks. The hooks allow the seed to be caught on animals' fur or on people's clothing.

butt plate: On a musket or rifle, the metal plate covering the end of the gun that is held against a person's shoulder. The plate helps cushion the impact of the gun on the user's body when it is fired.

carbon black: A material made of carbon, such as soot left by a fire, used to add color to ink or paint.

carpetbag: A bag made of carpet and used by travelers, much like a modern suitcase.

cataract: A large and steep waterfall or rapids in a river.

Chief Turkeyfoot: The last stand of Chief Turkeyfoot is a legend, which may or may not be true. None of the twenty eyewitness accounts, written shortly after the Battle of Fallen Timbers by participants in the battle, mentions any Native American taking a last stand on a rock during the battle, nor do any of the accounts mention a chief by the name of Turkeyfoot. However, the story has been told since at least the 1840s, and many Native Americans leave tobacco on the rock in Fallen Timbers State Memorial Park in order to honor the chief's memory.

cholera: A disease transmitted by bacteria in drinking water that causes severe diarrhea and dehydration. In Sims's time, the disease was often fatal.

cordwood: Cut wood stacked for storage.

corner marker: A marker used to indicate the boundaries of a piece of land.

cradle knoll: A rounded area in the earth left by an uprooted tree.

dandy: A negative term for a man who appears to not be interested in serious matters and who places importance instead on fashion and leisure.

doubletree: A bar to which two animals may be harnessed in order to pull a wagon.

dulcimer: A stringed instrument played by plucking and strumming the strings. The instrument is placed flat on the musician's lap and played from above, rather than held against the body like a guitar. Today it is often called an Appalachian or mountain dulcimer because it was brought to the United States by early immigrants to the Appalachian Mountain region.

flagon: A container for beverages, usually made of metal or pottery and including a handle, spout, and lid.

flapjacks: Pancakes.

flatboat: A square-cornered boat with a flat bottom used for transporting cargo in shallow waters.

flintlock: The part of a gun containing a flint used to strike a spark and ignite the gun's charge.

frizzen: A steel plate in a gun that is struck by the flint, creating the spark that ignites the gun's charge.

frock coat: A man's knee-length suit coat.

furlong: A unit of distance measuring 220 yards.

gum Arabic: Tree sap or resin used in the making of ink, specifically from the acacia, or gum, tree.

hardtack: A saltless hard biscuit or cracker.

herbal: A book used for identification of plants and their medicinal properties.

hoecake: A type of cornbread, so called because it often was cooked on the blade of a large garden hoe held over a fire. This method of cooking was common among slaves in the cotton fields of the South.

homestead: The land on which pioneers chose to settle.

hostler: A person employed in a stable to take care of horses and mules.

Indian wrestling: A type of wrestling in which two people lie side-by-side on their backs, entwine their legs, and try to flip the other over. The name comes from the belief that this was a Native American sport.

iron salts: A form of iron used to make ink permanent, unable to be washed away or dissolved.

keelboat: A type of shallow boat that is covered and used for carrying cargo.

larder: Another term for pantry, or a place in which to store food.

lean-to shack: A small, roughly built shelter with a single slope to the roof.

livery: A stable offering horses, wagons, carriages, etc., for rent. Liveries also would board horses for a fee.

malaria: A disease transmitted by mosquitoes that causes attacks of chills and fever.

mollycoddle: To treat someone with a large degree of attention or indulgence.

Mon Dieu: A French expression meaning "My God."

mortar: A bowl in which material can be ground into powder with a pestle.

mumblety-peg: A game in which players try to flip a knife so that its blade will stick in the ground.

musket: A gun with a smooth bore inside the barrel.

n'est-ce pas: French, meaning "Isn't it? or "Isn't that right?"

no truck: To have "no truck" with someone means to not trust or want to deal with that person.

offal: The internal organs and other waste discarded when an animal is butchered.

Orangeman: An Irish person who is a Protestant.

paint: A horse marked with patches of white and another color; also called pinto.

pallet: A small platform used as a temporary bed, sometimes including a straw-filled mattress.

pan: The part of a gun that transmits the spark to the gunpowder, firing the gun.

parasol: A small umbrella usually used to provide shade from the sun.

pemmican: Meat that has been dried, pounded thin, and usually mixed with melted fat.

pestle: A small club-shaped tool used to grind or pound material in a bowl-like vessel called a mortar.

portage: To carry a boat overland to avoid an obstacle (such as a waterfall or rapids) in a river.

possibles bag: A small bag with a strap often made of leather used to carry items such as food and ammunition while traveling.

poultice: A soft, moist, medicinal material heated and spread onto a cloth. The cloth is placed on the skin in order to treat pain or swelling.

powder horn: A container made of an ox or cow horn and used for carrying gunpowder.

ragamuffin: A poorly dressed, dirty child.

railing: Scolding or speaking unkindly.

ramrod: A rod used for placing the charge in a muzzle-loaded gun.

repast: A meal.

schooner: A type of sailboat used to carry people and cargo.

shanty: A small, usually wooden shelter or house built quickly and roughly.

shillelagh: A short, heavy club.

shot: Ammunition made up of small lead or steel balls.

side pork: Bacon.

smallpox: A disease that creates painful, fluid-filled blisters all over the body.

spigot: A faucet.

spring beauty: A wildflower with small pink flowers.

squatter: A person who settles on a piece of land without owning or paying rent on it.

stovepipe hat: A man's tall top hat, so called because it was shaped like a stove's chimney. Abraham Lincoln was famous for wearing such a hat.

sumptuous: Very large, expensive, and grand.

sweep: A large steering oar on a flatboat, controlled by a person standing on the roof of the flatboat's cabin.

sweetgrass: A fragrant type of wild grass often used in making baskets.

tarpaulin: A piece of material (often cloth) used to protect or cover exposed surfaces.

tinder: Flammable material used to start a fire.

tinderbox: A box used for holding tinder in order to keep it dry.

towhead: A term for a person with light blond hair resembling the color of flax.

trade goods: Items used instead of money for buying and selling things.

trigger guard: A loop surrounding a gun's trigger that prevents the gun from firing accidentally.

Underground Railroad: A network of meeting points and safe houses led by sympathizers of fugitive slaves who helped transport the slaves to freedom in the northern United States and Canada.

veranda: A porch.

vittles: A term for food.

water wagon: A wagon with a large tank for carrying water.

wedge: A metal, triangular-shaped tool used to split logs. When hit with a hammer or mallet, the wedge forces the log to split apart.

will-o'-the-wisp: A flickering light often seen at night over a bog or marsh. The light is created by the ignition of "marsh gas," the methane gas produced by the breakdown of plant and animal matter in water.

Acknowledgments

In the years since I first heard the story behind this book, many people have assisted in its completion. I would like to thank some of them, aware of the danger of leaving someone out.

Chloeann Jones is the person who first told me about the story and took me to Tiptonville and the Fulton County Museum. I told her story to the late Wiley Spurgeon, a Muncie, Indiana, historian and writer. It was he who suggested that I write the story as a historical novel for young people. My friend Dave Blimm got together the first research notes.

There were those who helped me on a regular basis as situations arose for which I needed help. Patricia Cornwell and her husband John did their part to keep me on task. Novelist James Alexander Thom furnished both encouragement and insight into Native American cultures. Writer Earl Conn and I communicated regularly throughout the entire process.

I would be remiss not to mention some of the libraries and museums that contributed. The Logansport Public

Library and the Cass County Historical Society were instrumental in providing information about the area during the time frame of the story. At the Allen County-Fort Wayne Historical Society Museum I found what I needed to know about Jean Baptiste Richardville and Johnny Appleseed. The public libraries in Defiance, Napoleon, and Grand Rapids, Ohio, had local historical information waiting for me when I arrived. Staff members at Historic Sauder Village in Archbold, Ohio, generously provided insight as to what life was like in the Black Swamp at the time.

Former Indiana Historical Society Press assistant editor Judith Q. McMullen suggested that I submit the story. Special thanks must also go to other personnel at the IHS Press for all their hard work. Intern Evan Gaughan selected the initial illustrations, and intern Wendy L. Adams proofread the final manuscript against the typeset book. Assistant editor Rachel M. Popma worked patiently with me on the early edits, and Teresa Baer's editorial insight and historical knowledge fine-tuned the book.

Then there were the friends and relatives who listened patiently over the years as I told them the story that many of them had heard several times before. Noteworthy among these is Pete Yohler, now a retired elementary school teacher, who read the early drafts to his students.

Selected Bibliography

All Web sites listed below were accessed in February 2008.

Books

Buley, R. Carlyle. *The Old Northwest: Pioneer Period, 1815–1840*. 2 vols. Indianapolis: Indiana Historical Society, 1950.

Carmony, Donald F. *Indiana, 1816–1850: The Pioneer Era*. Vol. 2 of The History of Indiana. Indianapolis: Indiana Historical Bureau and Indiana Historical Society, 1998.

Cooke, Sarah E., and Rachel B. Ramadhyani, comps. *Indians and a Changing Frontier: The Art of George Winter*. Indianapolis: Indiana Historical Society and Tippecanoe County Historical Association, 1993.

Craig, Oscar J. *Ouiatanon*, in vol. 2 of Indiana Historical Society Publications. Indianapolis: Bowen-Merrill, 1895.

Dunn, Jacob Piatt. *French Settlements on the Wabash*, in vol. 2 of Indiana Historical Society Publications. Indianapolis: Bowen-Merrill, 1895.

Esarey, Logan. *A History of Indiana from Its Exploration to 1850*. Indianapolis: W. K. Stewart, 1915.

Gates, Paul Wallace. Introduction to *The John Tipton Papers*, comp. Glen A. Blackburn, eds. Nellie Armstrong Robertson and Dorothy Riker. Vol. 1. Indianapolis: Indiana Historical Bureau, 1942.

Hunter, Juanita. *Logansport and the Michigan Road*. Logansport, IN: Cass County Historical Society, 1990.

Kingsbury, Robert C. *An Atlas of Indiana*. Bloomington, IN: Indiana University Department of Geography, 1970.

Madison, James H. *The Indiana Way: A State History*. Bloomington and Indianapolis: Indiana University and Indiana Historical Society, 1986.

Powell, Jehu Z., ed. *History of Cass County Indiana: From Its Earliest Settlement to the Present Time*. Chicago: Lewis Publishing, 1913.

Rafert, Stewart. *The Miami Indians of Indiana: A Persistent People, 1654–1994*. Indianapolis: Indiana Historical Society, 1996.

Vonnegut, Emma S., trans. and ed. *The Schramm Letters: Written by Jacob Schramm and Members of His Family from Indiana to Germany in the Year 1836*. Indianapolis: Indiana Historical Society, 1935. Reprint, 1975, 2006.

Wilson, George R. "Early Indiana Trails and Surveys," in vol. 6 of Indiana Historical Society Publications. Indianapolis: Indiana Historical Society, 1919. Reprint as separate book, Indianapolis: Society of Indiana

Pioneers and Indiana Historical Society, 1972; reprint, Indianapolis: Indiana Historical Society, 1986, 1991.

Government Publications

Forest Preserve District of Cook County (Illinois). "Old Sauk Trail." Nature Bulletin 436-A. Dec. 4, 1971, on Newton Web site. http://www.newton.dep.anl.gov/natbltn/400-499/nb436.htm.

Hodge, Frederick Webb. *Handbook of American Indians North of Mexico*. Washington, DC: Government Printing Office, 1910.

Internet Sources

Allen County-Fort Wayne Historical Society. "Chief Richardville House." http://www.fwhistorycenter.com/chiefRichardvilleHouse.html.

Baker Creek Heirloom Seeds. "Baker Creek Heirloom Seeds Gardening Guide." http://rareseeds.com/guide/.

Bessert, Christopher J. "Historic US-16." Michigan Highways. http://www.michiganhighways.org/listings/HistoricUS-016.html.

Bob's Blackpowder Notebook. http://home.insightbb.com/~bspen/.

Conner Prairie. "American Indian Policies." http://www.connerprairie.org/HistoryOnline/policy.html.

———. "The Fall Creek Massacre." http://www.connerprairie.org/historyonline/fallcreek.html.

First People. "Treaty with the Potawatomi, October 27, 1832." http://www.firstpeople.us/FP-Html-Treaties/TreatyWithThePotawatomi1832c.html.

Foley, M. "Potawatomi Clothing." Foley Homepage. http://www.usd116.org/mfoley/pot/clothing.html.

Illinois Department of Natural Resources. "Starved Rock State Park: History." http://dnr.state.il.us/lands/landmgt/parks/i&m/east/starve/park.htm.

Illinois Historic Preservation Agency. *The Lincoln Log*. http://thelincolnlog.org/.

Illinois State Archives. "Record Group 952.000: U.S. General Land Office Records for Illinois." http://www.cyberdriveillinois.com/departments/archives/data_lan.html.

Indiana Department of Natural Resources. "Underground Railroad: Sites." http://www.in.gov/dnr/historic/ugrr_sites.html.

Indiana Historic Architecture. "Historic Landmarks of Fort Wayne, Indiana." http://www.preserveindiana.com/pixpages/ftwayne.htm.

Indiana Historical Society. "Indiana's Popular History: Levi Coffin." http://www.indianahistory.org/pop_hist/people/coffin.html.

Indiana State Archives. "Land Records Collection: Land Office Index." http://www.in.gov/icpr/3150.htm.

Karnes, Cyntia. "How to Make Ink." The Ink Corrosion Website. http://www.knaw.nl/ecpa/ink/make_ink.html.

Lake Manitou Association. "History of Lake Manitou."
http://www.lakemanitou.org/services.html.

Library of Congress. "The George Washington Papers
at the Library of Congress." The Library of Congress
American Memory. http://memory.loc.gov/ammem/
gwhtml/gwtime.html.

Madison-Jefferson County Public Library and Jefferson
County Historical Society. "River to Rail: The Rise
and Fall of River and Rail Transportation in Madison,
Indiana." http://rivertorail.mjcpl.org/.

Marshall County. "Chief Menominee Memorial."
Arealinks.net. http://www.arealinks.net/tourism/
menominee/index.html.

"Medical History." *History in Focus* 3 (Spring 2002).
Institute of Historical Research, University of London.
http://www.history.ac.uk/ihr/Focus/Medical/index.
html.

Mensch, Ann. "A Brief History of Early Settlers and
Settlement of Jasper County." Indiana Local His-
tory<−>Genealogy. http://home.att.net/~Local_
History/Jasper-Co-IN.htm.

Mni Sose Intertribal Water Right Coalition. "Prairie Band
of Potawatomi Indians Community Environmental
Profile." http://www.mnisose.org/profiles/pbpwatmi.htm.

The National Archives. "Records of the Bureau of Land
Management (Record Group 49) Held in NARA's
Great Lakes Region (Chicago, IL): Records of the

General Land Office, 1800–1908." http://www. archives.gov/great-lakes/finding-aids/land.html.

National Park Service. "Fort Necessity National Battle-field: The National Road." http://www.nps.gov/archive/ fone/natlroad.htm.

———. "Valley Forge National Historical Park: General Anthony Wayne Monument." http://www.nps.gov/ vafo/historyculture/waynemonument.htm.

Northern Illinois University. "Clothing and Appearance." http://www3.niu.edu/historicalbuildings/potawatomi/ clothing.htm.

Ohio Historical Society. "Fort Defiance." Ohio History Central. http://www.ohiohistorycentral.org/entry. php?rec=703.

———. "Toledo." Ohio History Central. http://www. ohiohistorycentral.org/entry.php?rec=808.

Polk, Bud. "Indiana Dunes: The Potawatomi." Native Languages of the Americas. http://www.geocities. com/bigorrin/archive37.htm.

Polke Mss., 1809–1868, collection guide. Lilly Library Manuscript Collections, Indiana University. http:// www.indiana.edu/~liblilly/lilly/mss/html/polke.html.

Pratt, G. Michael. "Battle of Fallen Timbers Was on Toledo Land." Fallen Timbers Battlefield: Archaeologi-cal Project at Heidelberg College. http://www2. heidelberg.edu/FallenTimbers/PressArchives/ FTBlade3-12.html. Reprint from *The Toledo Blade* (March 12, 1995).

Steinhardt, G. C., and D. P. Franzmeier. "Indiana Land Surveys, Their Development and Uses," in "Agronomy Guide." Purdue University Cooperative Extension Service. http://www.ces.purdue.edu/extmedia/AY/AY-237.html.

Sultzman, Lee, "Potawatomi History." First Nations. http://www.tolatsga.org/pota.html.

Wisconsin Historical Society. "Military Roads," in Wisconsin History Explorer. http://www.wisconsinhistory.org/archstories/early_roads/military_roads.asp.

————. "Treaty Councils, from Prairie du Chien to Madeline Island," in Turning Points. http://www.wisconsinhistory.org/turningpoints/tp-013/.

Periodicals

Aumann, F. R. "The Development of the Judicial System of Ohio." *Ohio History* 41 (1932): 195–236. Ohio Historical Society. http://www.ohiohistory.org/resource/publicat/.

Battin, Richard. "'Mad Anthony' Wayne at Fallen Timbers: General Wayne's Decisive Victory in the Northwest Territory Ends the Young Nation's Crisis of Authority." *The Early America Review* (Fall 1996). Reproduced from the *Fort Wayne News-Sentinel*, 1994–1996. Online on Archiving Early America, http://www.earlyamerica.com/review/fall96/anthony.html/.

Davis, Harold E. "Book Review: *Economic Basis of Ohio Politics, 1820–1840.*" *Ohio History* 47 (1938): 288–318.

Ohio Historical Society. http://www.ohiohistory.
     org/resource/publicat/.

"Document-Journal of an Emigrating Party of Pottawat-
     tomie Indians," *Indiana Magazine of History* 21, no. 4
     (December 1925): 315–36.

Gordon, Leon M., Jr. "The Red Man's Retreat from
     Northern Indiana," *Indiana Magazine of History* 46,
     no. 1 (March 1950): 39–60.

Graham, A. A. "The Military Posts, Forts, and Battlefields
     within the State of Ohio." *Ohio History* 3 (1889):
     300–11. Ohio Historical Society. http://www.ohio
     history.org/resource/publicat/.

"A History of Fishers and Geist." *Indianapolis Star*. Sep-
     tember 20, 2004.

Keheyan, Y., and L. Guilianelli. "Identification of Histori-
     cal Ink Ingredients Using Prolysis-GC-MS: A Model
     Study." *e-PreservationScience* 3 (2006): 5–10.

Lonn, Ella. "Ripples of the Black Hawk War in Northern
     Indiana," *Indiana Magazine of History* 20, no. 3 (Sep-
     tember 1924): 288–307.

Prather, Geneal. "The Struggle for the Michigan Road,"
     Indiana Magazine of History 39, no. 1 (March 1943):
     1–24.